SPEAKING WITH CARE

SPEAKING WITH CARE

HAWTHORN ACADEMY BOOK EIGHT

D.R. PERRY

THE SPEAKING WITH CARE TEAM

Thanks to our JIT Readers

Rachel Beckford
Dave Hicks
Veronica Stephan-Miller

Editor
SkyHunter Editing Team

LMBPN Publishing
PMB 196, 2540 South Maryland Pkwy
Las Vegas, NV 89109

Version 1.00, September 2021
(Previously published as a part of the megabook *Hawthorn Academy: Year Three*)
ebook ISBN: 978-1-68500-448-4
Print ISBN: 978-1-68500-449-1

CHAPTER ONE

The next morning, I went to the office before breakfast and requested an appointment with Ms. Khan, saying it was urgent. All through class, I figured she'd be too busy to see me, but on my way to the library, she stopped me in the hall.

"If you're not doing any critical research, I can squeeze you in, Aliyah."

"I've got time."

I followed her down the hall and out of the academic wing. Instead of the office, she brought me down the ramp toward the infirmary. A door I hadn't previously noticed opened off on the wall to the left of the infirmary's entrance.

The door wasn't here until this year.

The voice was right. I could feel it as I opened the door. As I passed through, I deliberately brushed against the frame and felt a tickling sensation like I had in Lab when Hal used space magic to borrow some sunlight. Inside, the room wasn't much larger than the one Logan used at Bubbe's. Except there wasn't a bed or even a desk.

Ms. Khan sat in a chair similar to the coveted comfy ones in the lounge. There were six more in a circle only incomplete to leave room for the door to open. While the one Ms. Khan sat in was neutral beige, the rest were each different colors, all vibrant instead of the pastel I'd so often seen in offices. Red, blue, yellow, green, white, purple. I sat in the blue one and spent a moment glancing around the room.

Instead of motivational posters or medical diagrams, these walls were hung with tapestries, again in multiple colors and geometric patterns. It gave a soothing effect without the blandness that usually came from more formal decor.

"They let me choose my trappings." She smiled. "How would you have decorated, Aliyah?"

"That's an interesting question." I sat up straight and thought about it. "The ocean. With sailboats and a wharf, like in town."

"Ah, the seaside is certainly a popular favorite." She nodded.

"What's another? Popular one, I mean."

"Well, mine's a frozen lake with skaters. That's unsurprising for an ice magus like me."

"So the ocean is a surprise from a fire or solar magus?"

"After twenty years' worth of answers, none quite surprise me." She sat back in her chair. "So, what brings you here?"

"First, I have to ask you a question to be sure I can speak freely." I paused, unable to properly phrase everything at first. "It's tricky."

"Okay."

"Last year, Dylan asked me to witness something for him. And this year. Well, if there'd been a counselor here, could he have come to them about it?"

"No." She shook her head. "Unless it was me. As his mother, I already knew about the test. I was under the impression you'd done yours over the summer, however."

"No, I asked to postpone it. It's coming up in a few weeks." I cleared my throat. "My grandmother said I ought to get into a routine to prepare, including counseling."

"She sounds wise."

"I left things a bit to the last minute though. Or maybe this is too soon. I'm sorry."

"Don't be. It's never too late to ask for help. Or too early. Especially when you know harsh terrain lies ahead."

"That's a relief." I leaned back in the chair and let the back of my head rest against the cushion. "Maybe the second one since my birthday. The test is brutal, and I'm afraid I might not come out, well, healthy on the other side of it."

"I've done some reading on the subject, and you're right to worry."

"Really?" I blinked. "That's not what I expected a counselor to say."

"I'd be doing you a disservice to dismiss a true concern, especially about a clearly risky ordeal." She shook her head. "Constant positivity isn't counseling. We're getting short on time, so I want you to make some lists. The things that worry you most for getting through the test, your biggest fears about what might happen afterward, and one list of things you're happy with about yourself now."

"That last one doesn't seem like it fits."

"Think of your version of soothing decor, Aliyah. The ships on the ocean. Don't they go out and encounter storms at sea?"

"Yeah."

"You included a wharf with your seaside. Why?"

"Because it's part of Salem, my home." I gasped. "Oh! The sailors need to know where home is."

"Exactly. So, work on those lists. I'll see you back here again tomorrow. Is there a better time than your library period?"

We figured out a schedule, with visits four days per week. By the time I headed back in time for Lab, I knew I'd made the right choice.

Mrs. Onassis showed up to Bishop's Row practice. Her familiar was a basilisk, but otherwise unlike Alex's in every way. Instead of green like Asceco, this one was purple and much larger, with fangs that protruded slightly past her lip scales. While Mrs. Onassis feigned indifference from the top of the bleachers, the basilisk watched me so intently that I shuddered a few times.

"Ignore Pharmaka, Morgenstern." Alex said while retrieving his ballistae from the equipment chest.

"A basilisk named remedy?" I blinked. "That's ironic."

"It's not." Alex adjusted the Velcro on his left wrist. "Double meaning, like a lot of Old Greek."

"What's the other one, then?" Dylan raised an eyebrow.

"Poison, of course." Alex rolled his eyes. "Anyway, like I said. Ignore her. She only gets worse if you pay attention to her."

"Like your mom." Grace snorted.

"Exactly." Alex cinched his cestus.

Grace blinked. Lena caught her eye and slowly nodded. When Grace opened her mouth, Lee put a finger over his lips.

"She sucks. Might as well own that." He shrugged. "Anyway, see you on the court."

He turned and jogged away, beginning a warm-up lap. Grace looked about as shell-shocked as I felt. Dylan patted the top of her head, then elbowed me.

"I think that's the most pleasant conversation our lot's ever had with the prince of darkness."

"Earl, not prince." Lena fished her equipment out of the chest.

"Same difference to this blue-collar boy." Dylan shrugged.

"His collar looks more cerulean every day." Faith stood from where she'd been leaning on the bottom bench. "If he's nobility and his mother's loaded, why's he working in the cafe?"

"He said it was none of my business when I asked," Lee offered.

"I think there's family trouble." I told them about the hearing, how Konstantin Onassis showed up with Alex to help him testify against Temperance.

"I bet it's one of those situations where the titled family went broke and married money." Faith took a casual glance over her shoulder and aimed a lazy grin at Alex's mother. "She knows my mom from way back. Logan's too. Debutantes all. So my guess is, he rebelled and she's cut him off to retaliate."

"Yeah." Lena nodded, then took off for her laps.

"Whoa." Dylan shook his head. "Like the evil version of you three." He indicated Faith, Grace, and me.

"Don't forget obscenely wealthy." Grace chuckled. "Because the three of us sure aren't."

"Two out of three," I corrected.

"Don't look at me." Faith did a few side stretches. "If all goes well, they'll write me out of the will."

"How does that mean going well?" Dylan asked.

"Wait and see." Her grin reminded me of a locked diary.

Coach Pickman ended our conversation with a blast on her whistle. We jogged out to run laps with Alex, doing our best to ignore his mother and her creepy basilisk.

"No Azrael?" Soda overflowed and splashed Dorian's sleeve. "Are you two okay, Grace?"

"We're fine." She handed Dorian a wad of napkins. "Gallows Hill has a craft fair that runs right over Parent's Night so I'm going stag. We'll meet up the next day off-campus."

"That's good." He dabbed at the spill, then mopped it up off the counter after he'd saved his blazer. "What about you, Aliyah? Who are you going with?"

"Hoo?" said Julia.

"Logan." My face heated up so I grabbed the sodden napkins and turned to toss them in the trash. "We've got, er, an agreement. About all the dances and stuff."

"Peep!" Ember stood up on my shoulder and flapped. Then she groomed the hair she'd blown out of place.

"Oh, right." Dorian chewed his lower lip, then opened his mouth and closed it again.

"Were you looking for a date?" I asked. "How about Dylan? He's not going with anyone."

"Not for me." Dorian shook his head. "I'm the DJ."

"Whoa! Congratulations!" Grace held out her knuckles for a fist-bump.

"Thanks. I've got some big shoes to fill, though." He sighed. "And someone to find a date for at the last minute."

"Right." I nodded. "Zeke's still staying in town."

"I know. I met up with him at your grandma's office to get his music files. Anyway, for a centuries-old vampire, he knows a lot about audio technology."

"Who are you playing matchmaker for, then?" Grace scratched her head.

"I'd rather keep that to myself for now." He set the fresh cup of beverage roulette on his tray and waved as he strolled away.

Grace let out a frustrated growl, and Lune stamped his foot.

"What's wrong?"

"Not knowing's going to bug me the rest of the week. Whoever it is, they were going with Dorian until he got tapped as DJ."

"We'll find out soon enough, I guess." I shrugged.

"Do you think it's Arick?"

"He's going with Hailey again." I grinned. "I think they're a couple."

"Lena?"

"A first-year guy asked her."

"Coach Pickman?" Grace wrinkled her nose. "Ew. Didn't mean to remind you of you know who."

"It's okay if we don't know, Grace. It's only a date."

"I want to help, is all." She sat, stirring her soup. "And see Dorian happy."

"I know. Look at it as a break. Social maneuvering's so last year."

"So's you and Logan being just friends, apparently."

"We are friends, though. In a bigger way."

"Really?" She raised an eyebrow.

"It's like Izzy says. There's no *just* about this friendship."

"I don't understand it, but if that's how you two want to do things, I'm in your corner."

"Thanks, Grace."

After lunch, I headed straight to Lab. We had time in the library, but I wanted to check on the plants we had growing for the end of the semester. They were a big part of the mid-term practical, where we'd use their roots to concoct a sleeping draught for familiars.

Inside at the teacher's bench stood a man I didn't recognize. The creature on the table was a different story. He sat on his haunches and tilted his head, bright blue eyes peering at me from a mask of red and white fur. He glanced at my shoulder and yipped. Ember flew off to join him, *peeping* good-naturedly.

"Hello, Zephyr."

"Hmm." The man closed Professor Hawkins' lab binder with one gnarled hand. "Miss Morgenstern, is it?"

"How did you know?"

"How else would you know my critter's name?"

"Good point."

"You're an overachiever, is that it?"

"No. Just interested in plants." I headed toward the trough that held my specimen, beside Dorian's. "I'm Aliyah."

"I'm informal." He grinned and shuffled toward the experimental garden in the window. "I'd like you to call me Hank, but that's not flying in here. So call me Mr. Thurston."

"Okay, Mr. Thurston."

"Aren't you surprised to see a trustee here?"

"Not really." I shrugged and examined a mottled leaf on the plant. "After last year… Look, I was in the room when magic with the power of a solar flare almost ashed the school. It's hard to believe it could be worse."

"A threat exists whether you believe in it or not." He shook his head, grin fading like blooms in frost. "Be prepared."

"Why?"

"You don't get to be my age by letting your guard down."

"Great." I sighed. "More danger. Exactly what we wanted."

"Keep your ears and eyes open, Miss Morgenstern."

"If it's so bad and you know about it, can't you say more? Or do something?"

"The people you've got to worry about are good at keeping their secrets. All this old air magus can do is show up. I'd rather be back on Block Island taking in the sea air."

"Okay." I nodded. "Anyone in particular I should watch—"

"Miss Morgenstern, please return to the library." Professor Hawkins stood at my elbow. "I've got to prepare the lab for class later."

"Yes, sir."

I collected Ember, who seemed dismayed about leaving her new friend, and headed down the hall where I sat with a botanical book until the bell rang. By the time Lab started, there was no sign of Mr. Thurston or Zephyr.

All week, I waited for Grace to bring outfits around like she had the year before. It never happened. She had the dresses and suits, but on Thursday she invited people to the room for them instead of dragging a rack through the hallways. Which was a good plan because there was no way she could have gotten it on the stairs. Somehow, she'd made garments for Lena and Arick too.

And Alex. She gave me ten minutes' warning before he arrived.

"Why him?" I asked with my back to her as I buried my nose in history notes.

"He's trying. I know what it's like, not being able to afford something decent to wear." She poked my shoulder and waited until I looked up at her before continuing. "Remember that dress you lent me our first year?"

"Yeah, but—"

"No buts. This is how I pay it forward."

"You're no moneybags."

"Neither were you. Didn't stop you. Anyway, I gave you the heads-up. You can take your homework to the cafe if you want to."

You don't.

"Whatever." I shrugged. "Mean people suck, nice people rule. Queen Grace forever."

"Thanks."

I couldn't fault Grace for paying it forward. Last year, doing the right thing had felt like an act of rebellion. Supporting a friend, doubly so. The main reason I stuck around was curiosity. I wanted to see what she'd made for him.

When Alex arrived, he mostly ignored me. His nonchalance was a relief. However, it didn't stick. He didn't indulge my curiosity either. Grace handed him the garment bag, which he unzipped only enough to reveal velvety purple fabric.

"It's beautiful."

"Thanks."

"You shouldn't have."

"I did for everyone else. Why not you?"

"Because." His voice cracked and his breath hitched. Then he said something too softly for me to make out.

"I don't care whether you wear it or not, but take it with you when you go. I don't have the room for it."

He walked toward the door, back stiff but shoulders shaking. He paused, and the tremors stopped. Alex turned his head and glared at me, but addressed my roommate.

"Not a word about this, DuBois."

"About the suit?" Grace raised an eyebrow.

"No, that's fine. Everything else, keep your mouth shut. Especially you, Morgenstern. Or else."

"Mum's the word." I narrowed my eyes.

"Nice double entendre. Remember it."

He pushed the door open and stalked out.

"Did you threaten him, Aliyah?"

"Back. He did it first."

"Oh yeah, he did." Grace sighed. "So much for mending fences. Anyway, did you want to see your gown?"

"I peeked in the bag already." I grinned. "Blue's an interesting choice."

"That's the overlay. Are you sure you don't want to try it on?"

"Nah. Your dressmaking is at epic levels. I trust you."

I finished studying while she left to shower. When she got back, I went to get cleaned up. By the time I'd done that, Grace had gone to sleep.

CHAPTER TWO

"Why can't we go down whenever?" Dylan shuffled his feet.

"We have to wait for the third-year music." Logan sighed.

"Meet the new rules, same as the old rules," Faith said. "That's all the headmaster cares about this year."

"Shh." Hal tilted his head toward the stairs. "It's starting."

"How you can hear the difference is beyond me." Faith sniffed. "I miss Zeke's pop waltzes."

"It's Voices of Spring, duh." Bailey rolled her eyes. "We get the fun stuff later, after introductions. Or don't you remember all those debutante balls?"

"Move it." Grace shooed her toward the stairs.

We got on two to a step with one in between, and Grace called for the lobby. The stairs moved more slowly than usual, and as we descended, Dorian announced us over the music through the PA under festive amber lighting.

"Feels like time travel," Logan murmured. "You look like a Gilded Age film star."

"Oh?" I blinked. "Like Marilyn Monroe?"

"Nah. She was only pretty."

I blushed, unsure what to say to that.

Fortunately, it was appropriate not to speak. We paraded across the dance floor in measured steps, like a procession or a living display. I would have felt embarrassed with all those eyes on me, but it was easy enough to imagine everyone gazed at Grace's handiwork.

Most of the third-years walked singly, with Hal and Faith and me and Logan the exceptions. The rest had dates, but not with each other and trailed off to meet them by the chairs at the sides of the dance floor.

Lee walked directly in front of us, his eyes glued to the door. When Izzy walked through it, he almost stopped in place. I didn't blame him. Grace had outfitted her, too.

Izzy's dress was sleek and red, a shade that complemented her deep bronze complexion. Instead of her usual braids or pigtails, she'd gathered her voluminous natural ringlets to one side, with a bright red hibiscus accenting a finishing touch. The moment he stepped off the parquet, Lee hurried to her side. Logan and I followed.

Bad idea.

At first, the inside voice's statement made no sense. A phoenix dove through the air like a comet toward Izzy. But Fifi was Elanor's familiar and friendly. As Ember launched from my shoulder and Doris hissed at Logan's heels, I realized my mistake. The plumes on the tail were blue instead of yellow, indicating this phoenix was older than the one I knew.

"Brand. Pattern eight."

The voice was brisk and clipped, exuding authority. The bird turned, inches from crashing into Izzy. He assumed a tight spiral over her head, and although no attack seemed imminent, the air shimmered above Izzy. Her hibiscus began wilting.

Banish some of that.

I clenched a fist and focused on damping down the heat. Logan tightened his grip on my other hand and the air immediately around us grew heavy with humidity. Lee put his hand on Izzy's shoulder. A moment later, the flower in her hair perked up, opening in full bloom. Scratch shook his head, loppy ears flopping from side to side as he sat on his haunches, whiskers twitching.

Logan gasped, still gripping my hand as he stepped slightly behind me, eyes averted. His posture reminded me of something. My mind shuffled through memories, but the train of thought derailed a moment later when Logan's father stepped into the middle of our group.

"Mister Young." He tilted his head back and glared down his nose. "You know outside guests aren't allowed at formal school functions."

"I got permission," he insisted.

"Yeah, I've got a letter and everything." Izzy reached in her bag and pulled out a bright yellow paper. Mr. Pierce took one glance at it and barked out something not quite a laugh.

"The headmaster hasn't informed us of any such request." Mr. Pierce narrowed his eyes.

"Does he have to?" Logan's voice shook and cracked like a sand-castle under a rising tide.

"Read the new handbook. And look a man in the eyes when speak-ing. You're such a disappointment. Like you were raised by wolves. As an Omega."

"Or dragons, perhaps." Professor DeBeer stepped between Mr. Pierce and us. "Have a closer look at that document."

Mr. Pierce glared at the paper as if he'd incinerate it.

"Why? Is it a forgery?"

"Nope. I signed it with the headmaster late this afternoon. Would you like to see my copy?" The bird on her shoulder opened and closed his beak, sending off blue sparks of lightning. "I'll gladly escort you to my office if so."

"No need." A man with chestnut hair gone gray at the temples stepped out of the shadows by the doorway. "Back down, Leo. It's authentic. At least precognitive psychics aren't undesirables."

"Thanks, Trustee Fairbanks." Professor DeBeer shot us a glance over her shoulder. "Anyway, this is a dance. Why not let the children go enjoy themselves?"

"Don't drench the ladies, son." Mr. Pierce glared at Logan, then snapped his fingers. Brand the phoenix swooped down to his shoulder, and the temperature cooled so suddenly it got foggy around Izzy's head. "Or you'll never get anywhere with them."

"Sorry," Logan mumbled. I felt him rein in the water he'd been conjuring.

"No worries." Izzy fluffed her hair. "Humidity's amazing for curls."

"Shall we?" Lee offered her his arm, and she took it.

We stepped onto the dance floor although Dorian was in mid-transition between the last song and the next. I didn't recognize what we danced to.

"What's this one?" I asked.

"*Perfect Day*." Logan sighed. "By Lou Reed. Ironic."

"How?"

"Wait until the end."

The song was short, and he was right. It faded out on a dark promise of reaping what's sown, and made me shiver. Logan gripped my hand and my waist tighter while leading us through the steps.

"Here's *Return to Serenity* by Testament." Zeke never announced songs, so I wasn't sure why Dorian did it now. "For everyone who needs it."

And they do.

The building magical tension on the dance floor palpably eased. Shoulders lowered, stances widened, and brows smoothed over. I felt bad for Dorian, though. Headmaster Hawkins appeared beside him a moment later, wagging one wrinkled finger in his face. Apparently, he'd violated some rule with those two sentences. The reprimand ended long before the song. Logan kept on dancing through the opening bars of *Black Letter Day* by The Cardigans, which Elanor had practiced almost all summer.

"Can we cut in?" Faith tapped my shoulder.

"Is that okay, Logan?"

"Um." He glanced at her, then Hal. "Okay."

I expected Faith to step in, but Hal did instead. We shuffled along somewhat in time with the music. Although my dancing had improved over the last couple of years, it was hard to get past my shock. Hal seemed more tired than I'd seen him all summer.

"You were right." He sighed down at me. Somehow, he'd grown again in the last week. At tryouts, he'd been a hair shorter.

"No. Not about how I did it." I shook my head. "Should have talked to you."

"Couldn't have. You had to decide right after tryouts."

"I could have given you a heads-up that night." I squeezed his hand. "I'm—"

"Don't apologize again." He squared his jaw. "Everybody does that now. The doctors down in Boston. Nurse Smith. Even Dad."

"I won't, then."

"Good. I'm sick, and it's nobody's fault except my cells. And bloody coincidence." He grinned. "I'm trying out UK cussing. The f-bomb felt too mundane, and I shouldn't have said it to you in the first place. So it's my turn to apologize. Sorry."

"It happens." I grinned back. "I'm glad you and Faith cut in."

"It was her idea. I wanted to corner you by the punch bowl."

"Don't look now, but Alex is spiking it again."

"Joy."

"I wonder if Logan can fix that." I glanced over my shoulder at Alex, who tucked the flask back in his purple velvet jacket and waved. "Detox it, I mean."

"Not until I've tried it." Hal dropped a wink. "I was serious about joy."

Oh. So it's like that?

"Why?" I asked my voice and my friend.

Bucket list.

No, I thought back.

Wait and see.

"I've never tried it. I'd like to, at least once."

"Well, okay then." I let him escort me off the dance floor. "I'm your designated driver."

"Thanks." He filled a cup, then raised it to me.

My eyes stung as he drained it and got another. Someone poked me in the back. I turned slowly so as not to attract any unwanted parental attention to Hal's underage drinking.

"Don't say a word, Morgenstern."

"Way ahead of you there, Prince Poison."

"Are we going to do this all the time?"

"Are we?" I raised an eyebrow.

"I'm trying to be...decent here."

"Spiked punch and ominous warnings aren't exactly normal overtures of friendship."

"What's normal, anyway? How you do it, or is variety allowed?"

"No. I mean yes." I took a step back.

"You don't even know." He shook his head. "Or believe me."

Is it so hard to imagine he's clueless?

"I believe you, Xan." Dorian tipped a ladle of punch into a cup. "Thanks for the drinky-drink. I've gotta go before the song changes."

"Xan?" I blinked. Dorian only rushed off without answering.

"Yeah, it's a nickname. Dorian's idea." Alex sighed. "Starting fresh, he says."

Xan. Try it.

"Why?"

"Never mind." He turned toward a stretch of empty wall, then strode away from us.

"Worked for Dorian." Hal hiccupped. "Different reason. But that's why."

"How many cups did you drink?"

"Dunno. It's good." Hal's grin was goofily lopsided. He finished the dregs.

"Okay, time to get you back to Faith."

"No. Water first, okay?" He glanced at the dance floor, where she and Logan glided around gracefully. "I couldn't keep up with her before."

"Let's sit, then."

I filled cups from the water cooler and sat with him, sipping.

"Wow." Hal chuckled. "It hurts less now."

"What hurts less?"

"Everything." He held his free hand out, opening and closing it. "Along with the mad energy I had aches, growing pains, all summer.

"Even on Logan's birthday?"

"Yeah. They got worse this week. Even with all the magic in here."

"Hey, have you talked to Bubbe lately?"

"No. Should I?"

"Remember what happened after we went to her office on Logan's birthday?"

"Oh!" His eyes widened. "She made phone calls."

"Right. Maybe she's heard something back by now."

"I might not want to know what, though."

I sat silent, trying not to make assumptions and screw up as I had with Alex. Or maybe Xan. Life on campus got more confusing by the minute. Curiouser, like I'd fallen through a looking glass.

"Hey, I want my future husband back on the dance floor." Faith held a hand out to Hal.

He took it, and they were off. He seemed more limber out there, despite his weariness. Maybe there was something to be said for removing pain from the complicated equation of his illness. "Wish I could do more to help him."

"Me too." Logan took my hand. "He drank punch by Alex, didn't he?"

"Yeah." I leaned my head on his shoulder.

"Good for him."

"I wanted to ask you to detoxify it, but he said no."

"Wouldn't have anyway." He leaned his head on mine. "Unless Hal asked me himself."

"He's like our leader this year, how Grace was last time."

"You think?"

"You don't?"

"No, I can't argue with your logic." Logan sighed. "I wish every-thing were easier for him, is all."

"Wish!" I sat up so fast our heads clunked together.

We both turned to face each other, checking for sore spots. He took both my hands in his once we verified we were unharmed.

"What's your eureka?"

"Wishes." I smiled. "Magic ones. You know the stained glass on the entrance to Academics?"

"Yeah. *Long Division*," he recited. "By Gamila Haddad-Hawk—" His eyes widened.

"His grandmother. In August, I found out she's a djinn. She's been gone, divided from the family. But someone on campus right now has her lamp. And after that, she's got one more turn left in it."

Logan gasped.

"Aliyah, you're a genius. If we find that lamp and get Hal mastery, he can wish away his illness."

"Doesn't work that way."

We looked up to see a woman who looked older than Bubbe standing over us. She was taller than me, but without the gangliness of my frame. Her plaited hair was entirely white, and her skin lightly dusted with amber freckles. A small brown bird with the same delicate carriage perched on the wide-brimmed hat she wore. I would have thought it a decoration if it hadn't let out three throaty chirring calls.

"Lamps can't cure disease?" He spoke to the bird, then put a hand over his mouth. "Oops. That was bad manners, talking to your familiar like you aren't even there."

"You must be Logan Pierce."

"Yes, ma'am." He stood and bowed. "And you're Duchess Georgina Dunstable, of the Queen's court. From Marblehead."

"Duchess no longer, but the rest is true." She nodded.

I stood.

"Marquess?" he asked. A *faux pas* when talking to full-fledged Faeries, retired or not.

"I can't imagine why he's so interested, Miss."

"I'm Aliyah Morgenstern." Now I curtsied. "Aaron's and Angela's daughter. Mildred's granddaughter. Noah's great-niece." I kept my head bowed. "Richard Hopewell is my uncle."

"You may call me Georgia. One could say I'm retired."

"You can't retire from being a Faerie, I thought." I made it a statement instead of a question. Once changelings became Faeries, answering and asking them questions got tricky. Favors could come into play if we weren't careful.

"I was a magus first and graduated from Hawthorn Academy before the other side of my heritage made itself known. Under certain circumstances, mantles come and go. I completed my duties to Her Majesty and together with the king, she released me from court obligations to meet others."

"That's amazing!" Logan smiled. "You've got a rare set of circumstances. And a rare bird as well. Nightjars aren't usually magical."

"You are as well-educated as I've heard, Mr. Pierce. Your talents aren't exactly common either."

"Thanks." His smile faded. "So it's true that a lamp can't help Hal."

"Fern said it couldn't cure his specific illness, not that it can't help." The left corner of Georgia's mouth turned up. "Lamps are unpredictable and gaining mastery is no easy feat."

"If only someone knew where we should start," I commented.

"If only one were at liberty to say." She nodded. "I'm a wood magus. The walls have ears, among other things."

"I understand, Georgia." I grinned. "Thank you."

"Oh?" Logan blinked, then followed along. "Yes. Thanks for the chat. I kind of filled Aliyah's dance card for the evening and—"

"Say no more. I might be more of a recluse than the other trustees, but if the other students are as charming as the two of you, my habits may be due for some alteration. Perhaps I will entertain the idea of audits in the future, as time and space allow. Good evening."

We left her, stepping out on the dance floor as *Hallelujah* by Leonard Cohen played.

"What did all that mean?" Logan asked as we stepped along with the music.

"We have to talk about it off campus." I glanced to one side, where Mr. Fairbanks stood staring at me. "Too many enemies."

"Why can't people just be kind?"

"I don't know." I sighed. "Wouldn't the world be paradise if they were?"

We spent the rest of the evening dancing. As we ascended the moving staircase, we slipped our shoes off with sighs of relief. At least Logan's didn't have holes in them this time.

We said goodnight in the hall, halfway between our rooms. The hug was only awkward because of the shoes in our hands.

A large envelope, a legal-sized letter, and a package sat on my bed. The former was the application for Providence Paranormal College. The package had a return address from Harcourt Manor in Newport. The memory charm, which was an oval locket on a long chain. I tucked them both in my desk drawer.

I left the letter on my bed, waiting until I'd gotten into pajamas, used the restroom, and returned with a freshly scrubbed face to open it.

The stiffly formal text on the crisp beige page informed me that my extramagus test would take place on October fifteenth in the Hawthorn Academy Auditorium promptly at half past noon. I tucked the paper under my pillow, curled up under my comforter, and silently wept until I fell asleep.

CHAPTER THREE

Logan got a red marker and circled October fifteenth on the calendar he kept in his room, and in his planner. He even wrote it in the margins of his notebook. Every time I was in his quarters or studied with him elsewhere, the number fifteen stared at me like a baleful eye.

I kept waiting for my inside voice to admonish me, point out that I could have done this the easy way. It didn't. A few days before the test, as I ran laps in the gym by myself, I asked it why.

Because you're doing the right thing. This can't continue, and Hopewells have always been catalysts to change.

"Didn't Richard hate the Reveal?" I gasped.

I didn't say they all like that feature of their coincidental landscape, but you must admit, he changed the world. So will you.

Why does it have to hurt so much, though? I thought my question this time instead of speaking to pace my run better.

Growth hurts.

I remembered the summer before my first year when I discovered I'd outgrown my bathing suit. The frantic sense of shame, the almost painful relief when Mom showed up with a new one. And bumping my head, elbows, and knees on everything for eighteen months before getting used to my height. *This will be worse. I'm submitting to torture. Then sending out a recording of it.*

Yes. It's the right thing.

Some people will laugh. Or worse. Say I deserved it.

Maybe more will rally against such cruelty.

Maybe I should leave the memory charm under my pillow. Let someone else do this.

That's your choice, but nobody has so far, not for centuries. Not even dragons, who live for eons.

I stopped running and leaned over with one hand on my knee and the other on my gut. I struggled to stay on my feet as dry heaves wracked my body. Staggering, I made my way to the bleachers, sat, and sobbed with my head in my hands.

Nobody came to my rescue. The gym remained empty and silent. The solitude felt like a blessing, time and space to recover from the enormity of what I meant to do. A pause, if not a moment of peace exactly.

I stood and went upstairs to my room, then the baths. Faith swam, and we greeted each other briefly. Ember played with Seth as I showered and prepared for bed. Back in my room, Grace studied. Our syllabi finally aligned this year, so I took some time to discuss the reading on Faerie courts with her.

"I get that the Monarchs only reconciled recently, but how did they ever maintain balance between their courts when she had the only navy?" Grace tapped her pencil against her textbook.

"The King had practically an armada of pirates, mostly trolls. I thought you knew about that since you spent two summers in town and the Pirate Festival happens every August right here on Essex Street."

"Guess I'm more of a workaholic than you knew, eh?" She grinned. "So, pirates. Were they organized like in mundane Elizabethan times?"

"Yeah. They have ranks and everything. Az says they were like a militia with ships."

"Oh! I should pick his brain on this subject over coffee. Maybe in a couple of days. Want to bring Logan and make it a double study date?"

"Oh, I'm not sure." I turned down my bed, a reasonable excuse to put my back to her. "I have to ask. Don't remember cheer squad's practice schedule."

"Okay. You okay? This is early for you to turn in."

"Hard workout at the gym."

"Okay, I'll finish studying in the lounge." She scooped up her text and notebook and tucked her pencil behind her ear. "See you later."

"Yeah. Goodnight, Grace."

After the door closed, I turned out the light and lay in bed trembling. Sleep eluded me until Ember curled up in the crook of my neck and crooned softly in my ear.

The hardest part wasn't watching Nurse Smith come in and take Ember away to be sedated. It wasn't walking down the hall toward the auditorium. Or remembering to activate the memory charm outside the door. It wasn't even Director-General Rockport standing like a stone as I entered that glass and metal box or hearing his monotone incantation of the elements.

Leaving my friends in the cafeteria, called on and teleported away by Professor Hawkins was hardest. They all assumed I'd gotten myself into trouble, something I'd kept to myself. The last mind's-eye image of the people I counted on included disbelief, shock, and even suspicion. If Dylan realized what was going on, his face didn't show it.

That indignity only amplified the entire ordeal because I couldn't lean on remembering Grace's kindness, Faith's resilience, Dorian's sass, or Hal's righteousness. Instead, after the darkness that compelled me to conjure light and the arctic blast that invoked my fire, I had nothing to lean on.

Oh, but you do. Front and center.

I looked out and found my candle on the water.

Logan Pierce sat in the front row. I couldn't tell you who sat beside him because they didn't matter to me. Only he stood out, clutching his notebook to his chest with tears glowing on his cheeks as though he'd conjured instead of shed them. A sharp spike of guilt made me gasp. He'd broken before I had.

No.

I looked again and realized my error. Logan wasn't breaking. When he started rocking in his seat, I understood. His tears were a valve, releasing pressure. While the trustees looked at him sideways, especially his father, the rocking helped him cope with what he saw.

Which was me, stuck in a cage while it filled with water I couldn't banish or conjure air to counter. I clutched my throat, willing myself not to scream and lose precious air. Or worse, let water into my lungs. The last thing I wanted to do was vomit on film. Or the next best thing.

The water vanished, replaced by nothing. Not even air. That's when I realized my test was different than Dylan's, more comprehensive. I stood in a vacuum, spots of gray invading my field of vision.

Good. Let them do their worst for everyone to see.

They did. I was on my knees, barely able to get back up when I felt my arms and legs displace themselves. Not like dislocation, which I'd done to my shoulder when I was eight and fell out of the mulberry tree in the backyard. They flickered, like Hal's fists when we almost fought over Bishop's Row.

They're using space on you.

I screamed, knowing Logan, the faculty, and the trustees couldn't hear. The sensation of flickering in and out of existence was so horrifying I'd nearly forgotten the memory charm. How could Hal stand it?

Just a moment more.

The phasing stopped, and I shivered uncontrollably until a disturbingly familiar swooning sensation came over me.

Poison. You know what to do.

I burned it out of myself easily, hands flaring with flames as my magic did its work. Now, that grin felt a million times more genuine.

It vanished a moment later when my head filled with a cacophony of traffic noise, fire alarms, and air raid sirens. I held my hands to my ears, shaking my head, but could find no relief. I didn't understand. Sound manipulation was a psychic power. I almost panicked, thinking they were trying everything on me, beyond the limits of even extramagi.

It's mind magic.

I wish I could have relaxed with that knowledge, but too much noise, even inside my head, was impossible to ignore. And it got worse. A voice joined in. An outside one.

Save the world.

I did not say that.

Kill yourself.

Don't.

You almost did last year. Don't give up on giving up.

No!

I dropped to my knees, screaming, my head feeling like it had been impaled on an iron spike, that it'd split open any moment. With palms to temples, I tried to banish that other harsher voice and the noise that must have let it in.

Dylan endured. You can too.

Ram the glass, nose-first.

Be still.

And you'll die.

Live.

And never have to hear any of this again.

"Get out of my head!"

No.

I was never only in your head. Keep fighting.

I'd either lost the ability to form words or had nothing left to say, but I listened to the voice. My voice, the one with me through my entire time at Hawthorn. The one that helped me save Logan and Noah. I felt worn out, spread thin, practically flattened. My voice was like a live wire, a conduit, my connection to something bigger.

Hold on.

The image of a rope hanging down from a cliff face came unbidden to my mind's eye. I imagined myself grasping it and clinging, but I didn't move up or out of the miasma that filled my senses. Not until I tugged.

Let go.

"No. Get out!"

I kept pulling. That imaginary rock face moved. No, I did. Until it blurred beside me and air moved in the wake of my passage. I opened my eyes to find that nothing like that was actually happening.

The noise cut off mid-wail.

Director-General Rockport stood staring at me. One glance at the audience confirmed my suspicions. I'd shocked them all, especially Mr. Fairbanks, whose face was an alarming shade of crimson. Except for Logan whose lips tilted up, hinting at a grin. His eyes glanced to one side. I finally recognized where I'd seen that before.

Azrael's chess set, I thought. He—he was the King. And I—

The chamber opened behind me, and I passed out.

"—no idea she—"

"—as rare as mind—"

"—couldn't have known—"

"—could be null instead—"

I tried banishing those voices like I had the one advocating suicide. It didn't work. Moments later, I understood why. They were in my ears, not my head. My hand didn't move when I tried lifting it because it was tangled up with someone else's.

My eyes opened on Logan, the light around the back of his head like a halo.

"Angel." The voice croaked.

"I'm Logan." He blinked. "You're alive, not in heaven."

Explaining was impossible until he held a cup of water with a straw in front of my mouth. I sipped, swallowed, repeated.

"You look like one."

"Oh." He blushed. "Same. Except you're, uh, lying down."

Something soft that vibrated rubbed against my hand. I glanced down to see Doris, tail slightly twitching as she purred on my stomach. I looked around for Ember and saw her asleep in a basket on the bedside table, her side rising and falling in time with her tiny snores.

"What happened?" I glanced at my other side and saw the head-master sitting there with Nurse Smith.

"The official answer is fire, solar, and an as yet unknown ability. Inconclusive." He raised an eyebrow. "Perhaps you can tell me."

"I don't know." I groaned. "I'm exhausted."

"It'll be at least a week before she fully recovers, sir." Nurse Smith took my wrist in his hand, checking my pulse. "Maybe two."

"You'll have to figure it out by All Saint's Day and have proof you're telling the truth." The headmaster's lips pressed together in a bloodless line. "Or go through a second round of testing next month."

My eyes teared up immediately, and I wept. I'd never experienced such a hat-drop emotional reaction before in my life. But then, I'd never been through anything as harrowing as that last round of the test.

"Hiram! How could you?"

I blinked and looked around. The owner of the distinctly feminine voice wasn't in the room. Hal stood in the doorway, looking about as confused and worn out as I felt. Faith stood on his other side, her arm out in case he needed it. On her other, Seth and Nin rode in a tote bag.

"Grandpa. You're too harsh." He shuffled over and sat on the bed across from mine.

"It is, however unfortunately, true." He sniffed. "You shouldn't be here, Harold."

"Infusion time, Gramps." Hal smirked. "By appointment. Check the schedule."

"Miss Morgenstern, you know what I require." The headmaster straightened his tie. "Report to my office with it on November first." He turned and left the room.

All three of us waited until the tap of leather-soled shoes on tile faded away. Faith sat in the chair at Hal's bedside while Nurse Smith started the IV line leading from the wall. Once he finished, he closed the door as he left to give us all privacy.

"You didn't start up last winter's exercise regimen again, Aliyah?" Faith raised an eyebrow. "You look like—well. Like you tangled with my sister again."

"No." I patted my shirt just over the breastbone and found the memory charm still there. The next time I went home, it'd be going in the postage-paid box back to Blaine and Kim in Rhode Island, where they'd extract the psychic impressions. "I can't say exactly, but you'll find out soon."

"Okay?" Faith blinked.

"She tangled all right." Hal shook his head. "Alone but with an audience, somehow. I can't figure out how or why, though."

"You used your magic to spy on us?" Logan's nostrils flared.

"I've known something was up for a week now." Hal sighed. "The same thing that I couldn't figure out last fall with Dylan."

"Why?" I cleared my throat. "I mean, why go to all that trouble, checking on me?"

"We're friends, aren't we?"

"Plus, he's nosy." Faith snorted. "Always has been."

"You love me anyway." He grinned.

"You might not be perfect." She took his hand in both of hers. "But you're perfect for me."

Someone knocked on the door. Seth barked and wagged his tail. Logan grinned at the sha.

"It's Dylan. Do you guys want him here?"

We all nodded, and Logan let him in.

"Hey." His hands were full with a tray of beverages so Logan closed the door behind him. "Smoothies don't fix everything, but they definitely help. So I figured I'd bring some."

"Thanks." I looked him in the eyes as he handed me a purple concoction. "Is this what you drank?"

"Last year, yeah." He nodded. "Ginger and elderberry for you. Hal's is orange coconut." Each cup was marked with a name in silver sharpie, but not Dylan's handwriting.

"How did you know what I drink on infusion day?" Hal asked after a sip of his orange-tinted smoothie. "Did you make these?"

"No." Dylan had his back to us, trying to coax Gale away from Ember's basket. He was trying to get in with her, but there wasn't much room. "I went to order something, and they were already there."

"Let him stay," Logan said. "She's still zonked from the sleeping draught."

"Yeah." Dylan let the dragonets be and paced the room. "It took Gale over an hour to wake up from that."

"So the same thing *did* happen last year." Hal sighed. "I knew it."

"You're not supposed to know." Dylan handed Logan a vanilla smoothie and took the green tea one for himself. "Nobody but us chickens." He gestured at Logan and me with his beverage.

"It's got to be because you're both extramagi, but I can't figure Logan's part in it." Hal glanced at each of us in turn.

We sat silently.

"Look, somebody important gave me an ominous warning recently." Logan leaned back in his seat. He pointed at the wall, then his ears.

"Let's go out this weekend." Faith nodded. "It's been a while since we all hung out in town, and Halloween stuff is everywhere right now. It'll be fun."

"I've got a gig on Friday night," Dylan said.

"That's good." I grinned. "It'll be nice to see everyone. Where are you playing?"

"Out on the Common. Part of Haunted Happenings, thanks to our Ambersmith connections. We're going to want food afterward. Engine House?"

"I'd like someplace quieter. Um." I cleared my throat and made a show of rubbing my temples. "In case this headache isn't totally gone."

"I'll talk to the band. We'll figure it out." Dylan nodded.

"Peep?" Ember lifted her head and bumped it against Gale's.

"Broo?" Gale thumped his tail against the outside of the basket and put a wing over her.

"Peep." She settled back down.

We all did too, drinking our smoothies and letting Faith point the conversation at cheer squad and Bishop's Row. We'd discuss the serious business over the weekend.

CHAPTER FOUR

Piercing Whispers played mostly covers, classic spooky numbers like *This Is Halloween* and *Strange Magic*. However, they closed out their set with their hyped-up version of *Groovy Kind of Love*. They'd turned it into *Spooky Kind Of Love* and doubled the pace. The crowd loved it. After the opening number, I wasn't part of the throng that made me feel claustrophobic despite the outdoor venue. Hal sat with me on the swings at the playground in the far corner of the small park.

"I don't have the spoons for that." He gestured.

"Spoons?"

"Sorry. I learned it a while back, but it hasn't slipped out around you all until now. It's a way to measure energy. How much you have left to use once whatever ailment takes its share."

"How does that work?"

"Well, think of it this way. When you wake up in the morning, you're pretty much rested. For people like me, that's not a sure thing."

"So it's like choosing your battles?"

"I wish." Hal sighed. "More like choosing whether to go all the way to the bathroom to wash my face or use the grooming station in my room."

"It's that bad?"

"It was worse last year than it is now, but not way worse." He hung his head. "Faith grooms Nin every week now because I never have the spoons."

"How can I help?"

"Well, there's one thing." He looked up. "I invented a device that'd help me, but I'll never get it done alone."

"Whatever you need for that, consider it done." I grinned. "Even if it's other people enchanting things. I'll herd those cats."

"Thanks. I'm making myself a magipsychic moving chair. One that fits on the stairs." He chuckled. "Match my rhyming if you dare."

"Strong enough to lift a bear?" I snickered. "Perhaps a pair?"

We sat there rocking in the swings and laughing so hard I feared we'd fall out of them. Almost.

"Are you done?"

I stood immediately and turned as Hal tried to catch his breath. My hands held out in front of me, dukes up, glowed enough to reveal the speaker's identity.

"Crow?"

"Get out of here." Something sharp gleamed in his hand and he took a step toward me.

"This is a public place."

"It's also my turf, and I've got business here. Scram." He held the object up, leaving no doubt it was a knife. A punch dagger, to be specific, a nasty sort of weapon. I'd seen Bubbe care for critters wounded by those.

"He needs a minute." I jerked my chin at Hal, not daring to lower my hands.

"He's got ten seconds."

"Or you'll do what?" My hands glowed brighter. "Make me melt that blade?"

"Think you can flame hot enough to melt Damascus, extranutcase?"

"If that's Damascus, I'm the Goblin King." Hal snorted. "Anyway, we're gone. Come on, Aliyah. He's not worth it."

I saw him stumble and almost turned away from the knife-brandishing shifter to catch him. However, someone else did—a girl, short but strong enough to support Hal's new and improved bulk alone. With one arm, I noticed as she gave me a thumbs up with the other.

"Cadence will hear about this, Crow." The girl spoke airily, as though this was a game to her. Or routine.

I backed away, somehow following Hal and his rescuer again without looking at them.

"Like she'll believe you, kid." He stepped into the shadows under the slide.

Although punch daggers weren't balanced for it, I waited until we were out of throwing range before turning around. I banished the fire and got a better look at the girl helping Hal, who looked familiar but I couldn't recall her name. She was about Grace's height with black hair falling in untidy waves around her face. Her clothing was a strange mix of too big for her and too small. While her ankles stuck out awkwardly from the hem of ragged jeans, she practically swam in her pullover sweatshirt.

"Where'd you come from?" Hal asked.

"Around. I'm local, like you. You've got the biggest balls I've ever seen. Figuratively. I'm still only allowed to watch PG-13 movies if there's sex in them."

"I'm Hal. What's your name?"

"Mavis." She sighed and I remembered. I'd met her at the college fair. "Merlini. Sorry about my brother. He's jerkier than an entire case of Slim-Jims."

"Crow's your brother?" Hal blinked.

"Misfortune is my birthright, yes." She nodded. "And I'm an enormous tattletale. The best, in fact." She patted the pocket on the hooded sweatshirt she wore. It chimed. "Cadence already knows about these shenanigans. That's my read alert."

"Red alert?" I blinked.

"No, read like a book, not roses." She giggled. "Danger, Cadence DelMar."

"I get that reference." Hal chuckled.

"For a dude challenged by walking, you've got a good sense of humor, Hal."

"Where are you taking us anyway?" I didn't exactly trust Mavis Merlini, even if she was Cadence's pal and momentarily helpful.

Good call. She has an agenda. Maybe if you pushed you'd discover it. Or something about yourself that you need to know next week.

I swallowed, unsure whether to follow the voice's advice this time. It had been correct usually, and mostly on my side, but I refused to experiment with mind magic on an unwitting and unwilling person. That was the point of meeting with my friends, after all. To ask for help. If I did this, I could harm an innocent girl and worry my friends for no reason.

Thanks but no thanks, I thought at the voice.

"That gate there." She pointed.

We reached it a moment later. Mavis waved and jogged away from us. Not toward the crowd, but not the playground either.

"Isn't she a little young to be out here by herself?" Hal asked. "Maybe you should go after her."

"She said PG-13, not PG." I shrugged. "If you want me to ask, I will."

"Please." He clung to the fencing with both hands. "I'd do it myself, but—"

"Say no more."

Mavis wasn't anywhere near as fast as me. I caught up with her easily, and she stopped.

"What's up?"

"We wondered if you needed someone to, I don't know, walk you home?"

"I'm fifteen. Didn't your parents let you wander around town in October at that age?" She tilted her head while peering at my *Shema Yisrael* necklace. "Ooh, that's pretty."

"Yes they did, but with friends. Thanks. It was my great-uncle's."

"I don't have friends."

"Other siblings then? They made me go around with Noah a lot."

"Look, Aliyah, I get what you're saying." She nodded. "I'm a lone wolf."

"We're people, not islands, Mavis. Do you want me to walk you home or not?"

"You really are as white-hat as Cadence says." She smiled. "Like a unicorn."

"They're mythological." I shrugged. "Which direction?"

"I'm not going home yet." She pointed toward Irzyk Park. "Take me to the tank. People are there who won't let anything bad happen to me, I swear."

"Okay." I pulled my phone out and sent a group message to everyone I'd come out with that night. "Let's go."

"What's it like, being an extramagus?"

"It kind of sucks most of the time. I scare people but don't like that at all."

"I get that." She sighed. "It's hard making friends when people are scared of you. How'd you do it?"

"It wasn't easy. The first day of school, I almost burned the cafeteria down."

"Get out!"

"It's true. But that guy you helped, Hal, he wanted to be my friend anyway."

"Is he your boyfriend?"

"No. That's Logan." I blushed. "Hal ended up with Faith Fairbanks."

"Then he's super courageous. Fairbanks." She snorted. "They're almost as scary as—well, as some people even I'm afraid of. So basically, when you're scary you have to let the brave people come to you?"

"No. Sometimes, it's laughing at the same things." I told her about Grace, how we shared a joke at the beginning, and that bond stuck.

"Well, I'm good at humor at least." She shrugged.

"Plus you're a shifter. That's always got a coolness factor."

"How did you know?"

"Lucky guess."

"Can you guess what kind?"

"A crow?"

"Wrong!" She blew a raspberry. "But you're close."

"Raven then."

"Damn, you're good."

"We're here." I jerked my chin at the defunct tank that made up the war memorial. A familiar pickup truck pulled up, and the window rolled down.

"Aliyah?" Bar stuck his head out the open window. "Oh, hi Mavis."

"Bartholomew Michael Angelino Micello!" She ran up to the truck's passenger side and tugged on the handle. "I said your true name! Now you have to drive me anywhere I ask."

"For the millionth time, that's not how changelings work."

"IHOP, pronto!" She got in the cab.

"No pancakes." He looked back at me. "What's going on?"

"Mavis helped Hal so I offered to walk her home. She said to take her here instead."

"Makes sense."

It didn't to me, but I was mature enough to understand that normal varied.

"Is Hal okay? Do you guys need a ride?" he asked.

"No, we were with more friends over on the Common. Piercing Whispers had a gig."

"Oh, cool. Are you all going for afters or anything? I'd love to see my pals from Hawthorn."

I didn't want to leave a friend stuck babysitting but couldn't invite him. Extramagus business was still secret business.

"No. But we'll all be at the masquerade ball on actual Halloween. Are Gallows Hill kids going?"

"Yeah, the whole crew from extramurals and then some." He grinned.

"So, we'll see you then. And at whatever afters happen."

"Sounds good."

We said goodbye, and I sprinted back to the gate on the Common. By the time I got there, Faith, Logan, and Piercing Whispers were all with Hal. Grace and Azrael had just walked up too. They'd already worked out a location. All I had to do was follow.

Elanor brought Arick and Azrael across the street with her, leaving the rest of us relatively alone in the apartment Noah shared with her.

"Get in." Noah opened the door to the soundproofed studio. "This is as private as it gets, but it might be a little crowded."

"It's not that bad. Just stay put." Hal sat on the bench behind the keyboard with Faith.

"So, what's this about?" Dylan raised an eyebrow at Hal.

"Don't ask me." He waved his hand. "This is not the fearless leader you're looking for."

"Dammit Hal, you're a space magus, not a Jedi mind trick." Grace chuckled. "Anyway, is this like an intervention or a support group or something? Because we're all in a circle and stuff."

I let go of Logan's hand and stepped away from the wall into the middle of the room.

"No. I'm coming clean to you all about something because you're my friends and you should know." Dylan opened his mouth so I spoke before he did. "Yeah, Dylan. A few of you already know some of this."

"Dish," Noah ordered. "Elanor can't stall forever."

I told them about the extramagus test, which entirely shocked Faith and Grace. Hal sat with his jaw clenched and his nostrils flaring. Noah and Dylan nodded through most of it, but even their mouths dropped open at the end.

"So, either I have to show proof of mind or null magic by All Saint's Day, or do the whole test again." I sighed. "And I don't know how."

"That's bullshit." Hal narrowed his eyes.

"It is. They should have checked her medical history." Faith twirled a strand of her hair between her fingers. "Especially to rule out null. Aliyah doesn't get migraines, and everybody knows null magi are practically plagued with them." She cleared her throat. "I might have studied a little too much on magical maladies." She mumbled something about alternative therapies and Providence Paranormal College.

"That makes sense." Logan nodded. "There are no documented extramagi in recorded history who had null magic. It might be impossible."

"So, how do we prove she's got mind magic, then?" Dylan asked.

"Mind works on line of sight." Grace grinned. "Aliyah has to be able to see us without knowing who's who. So how about a game of reverse hide and seek?"

"What's that now?" I blinked.

"We'll all be in costume at the masquerade ball, right? So, we keep our costumes a secret. That night, I hide myself and Aliyah with shadow magic. Then she tries to find you using her mind. Since she's hidden, nobody can give her unconscious clues. We should probably include some non-magi Aliyah can trust with this topic, like Izzy and Cadence."

"If we each start recording on our phones after Grace does her shadow thing, that's all the proof she needs." Logan clapped his hands.

"Okay, let's do this. I'll talk to Izzy and Cadence about it tomorrow." I looked around the room and watched everybody nod.

"One other thing." Noah drew a deep breath. "I might need your help, Aliyah. About my diploma."

"Sure. Anything."

"Hal?" Noah gestured at him. "You've got the info."

"So, a trustee named Andre Gauthier made the vote that expelled Noah last year. We want to talk to him, but he's a total recluse on campus. So, if this mind magic exercise is successful at the dance, do you think you could help us find him?"

"I'll do my best." I nodded.

After that, we all went back into the living room and hung around playing Mario Kart while eating convenience store snacks, saying nothing more about tests, games, or proof for the time being.

I slept at home that night and messaged Izzy and Cadence on Sunday. Only Izzy replied. We talked on a walk around the wharf, with liberal use of inside jokes and obscure references we'd shared since kindergarten. She agreed with Faith and was all in for the game, and said she'd get Cadence on board.

"How's she been?"

"A mess, to be honest." Izzy sighed. "She's not speaking to Crow. Says she never will after what happened on the common last night. How Crow threatened you and Hal. I flipped a few cards." She stared into her half-full cup of cider, then tossed it into the nearest trash bin without another sip.

"That bad, huh?"

"It's awful. He's worse than anyone could have guessed. Even with that stuff you and Grace overheard in the Lyceum kitchen last year."

"At least Hal and I can avoid him. What about Cadence? I'm worried he'll do something to her."

"Me too. The cards agree with us. But she says she's got it handled."

"Because of her mermaid's voice?"

Izzy nodded. "She didn't want to hear my reading."

"I learned way more than I wanted to last year about cruel people. They don't wait for people to defend themselves."

"Maybe she'll listen to a warning, coming from you. Want to take a spin by her place for a chat?"

"Yeah, let's do that." I tossed my cider too and we headed out of downtown toward The Point.

Nobody was home at the DelMar's apartment. Cadence didn't answer my calls or messages that day or any other I stepped off campus to make during the week. The following Saturday, Cadence sent me a picture of her folks doing an event at The Willows, along with the words "I'm in." After that, I didn't hear from her until the masquerade ball.

CHAPTER FIVE

No matter how many times I asked Grace about her costume for the masquerade ball, she gave me no straight answer. The only thing I knew for sure was that her outfit took up half her closet and that she used a box from a pair of boots to hold the accessories. I couldn't imagine anything as cool as the dragon costume she'd worn in the contest our first year, but she seemed far more excited about this one.

Grace didn't get dressed for the ball on campus. Instead, she brought everything to Azrael's and said she'd meet me there. That was fine with me. I wanted to mentally prepare for the reverse hide and seek game we'd be doing during the ball. Putting my costume on alone proved more challenging than I'd expected, however. I ended up trotting down the hall to find some help, but I was late.

Nobody was home at Faith's and Kitty's room, or Hal's and Lee's. Dylan and Arick were at Noah's because they were the opening act. I headed to Logan's, although the last thing I wanted to do was ask him to help me dress in case he thought I wanted something else. Talking with Bubbe had helped, but sexuality still confused me, and the inconclusive extramagus test results had distracted me from thinking more about it. That's why when I knocked on his door, I prayed that he wasn't there.

You know he's not.

He wasn't. I took a long shot and headed to the only other room on this floor that housed students and knocked.

"Just a minute!" Dorian called.

"Okay."

The door opened almost immediately after I spoke.

"Oh, you can come in." He grinned. "Thought you were Xan."

"Um." I stepped inside.

"We're walking over together." He closed the door. "For reasons."

"Are you two dating?"

"No. But there are reasons of a non-dating variety. Anyway, what's up with the bathrobe?"

I opened it and revealed the dark blue fabric, which sagged in ways it wasn't supposed to around my shoulders.

"Elsa? Not what I expected but cool. What's the problem?"

I turned and moved the white faux-fur trimmed hood and long braid away from the zipper. It ended in the middle of my back, between the tops of my shoulder blades, exactly where I couldn't reach.

"I can't fasten this by myself, and Grace went to Azrael's. I should have dressed at Bubbe's. Have you seen Logan?"

"He left with Hal and company." Dorian sighed. "His dad was looking for him, Faith said."

"Wow." I wrinkled my nose. "It's hard to get my brain around their families."

"Ditto. My parents are awesome. Kind of like yours, but without a kick-ass grandma downstairs. My Nonna's way older than Bubbe. She lives in a nursing home."

"Sorry."

"Thanks." He patted my shoulder. "Voila, you're a queen! Have a look."

He went to his wardrobe, opened it, and tilted the mirror on the inside of the door toward me. I loved how the nearly indigo blue looked with my hair and the way the silver diamond-shaped rhinestones glittered in the light. The shimmering mesh cape made me feel extra pretty. I did a little twirl and smiled until I noticed something missing from Dorian's reflection.

"Where's your costume?"

"I'm going, well sort of as myself, but wearing a mask." He crossed the room and opened the hatbox on his desk. "Check it out."

Before I got the chance, someone pounded on the door.

"Spanos, we gotta go!"

"That's my cue." Dorian gave me a sheepish grin.

Out in the hall, Alex glanced at me once and nodded. "Backup. Good idea."

I blinked, but both of them acted accustomed to this sort of talk. If that was the case, why did the two of them seem so nervous and in such a hurry? For all I knew, it was the regular dynamic in their strange friendship.

Not that strange.

I pondered the voice's opinion and decided to accept it. Hadn't I concluded last week that normal varied? I trotted to catch up with them again, not wanting to be the lone third-year student left on campus. Plus, I had business at the masquerade ball. Sitting it out wasn't an option. Alex practically jogged once I caught up. He couldn't run as fast as me, but it was a near thing. Poor Dorian struggled to keep up, breath chugging like a steam engine.

Once out the door, Alex grabbed our wrists and pulled us around the corner and into a shadowy alcove.

"Wait," he said, then let go of Dorian to put a finger over his lips.

I almost protested but started shivering instead. Ironic, given the character I'd dressed as. However, it wasn't the cold bothering me. Despite my confusion, I felt a clear and present fear. It struck me so unexpectedly that I didn't bother pulling out of Alex's grip. The urge to conjure an inferno or flee Hawthorn's entrance at top speed didn't feel natural, like this wasn't my idea.

It's not.

Dorian, who'd called himself a coward last year, stood in front of us with his mask under one arm. He pointed with his other hand at the cobblestone five feet from us, like he aimed a weapon. No, his magic. I couldn't figure out why until Alex whimpered beside me and I looked up. He'd grabbed Dorian's jacket and clung like it was a rope over a cliff.

Mrs. Onassis walked briskly away down Essex Street. She blended into the crowd a moment later, but Dorian and Alex waited, still uneasy.

"She's gone. We can—"

"No." Dorian shook his head. "Not yet. *He's* still coming."

"Think nothing," Alex whispered.

I blinked, considering that next-door to impossible. Especially after he told me not to.

Think Halloween.

Now that I could do. The sounds of excited costumed tourists, the aroma of cotton candy and popcorn wafting from food trucks, and the rich loamy scent of crisp autumn leaves underfoot already filled my senses. A childhood in Salem experiencing these every year let me magnify the experience until it drowned everything else out, even oddly-heroic Dorian and unexpectedly-cowering Alex.

I barely noticed when Mr. Fairbanks dragged Mr. Pierce along after him away from the door and into the crowd. He thought so loudly that I immediately knew he sought Alex, trying to pay back some sort of favor. A mind magus of his age and experience should have had no trouble, especially with how distraught Alex was. But he seemed entirely ignorant of our presence. I watched the back of his head grow smaller as he continued down the street.

Mental camouflage. You're doing it.

"What did you do, Morgenstern?" Alex whispered.

"I'm not sure."

"So you did do something." He let go of me and turned his head. "Uh, thanks. He found me every other time I tried going out."

"Wait, you haven't been off campus this whole time?" I blinked.

"His mom." Dorian shook his head. "But this is a masquerade. We thought, with costumes everywhere, nobody would know."

"Speaking of that." Alex pointed at the box. "We should mask up."

Dorian opened the box and handed a mask to Alex, who put it on and turned around. It gave him a grotesque visage, human but twisted so hideously I took a step back. That's when I saw Dorian's mask, a placid and beautiful but somehow masculine representation of a face. They were opposite but somehow similar although I couldn't determine how.

"We're Dorian Gray and the portrait of same." Dorian chuckled. "Cool, huh?"

"Wow. Well, nobody will recognize you, that's for sure." I nodded.

"Even so, would you happen to know an alternate route to the Hawthorne Hotel? Just to sort of make sure we avoid trustees."

"No problem."

I took them down Washington Street to Front Street, where we had to skirt the line for the Salem Wax Museum but otherwise walked without incident. At the door, we handed over our tickets. I noticed Alex's wasn't one given by the school, which meant he'd shelled out over a hundred dollars for it. At first, I wondered why but then realized only the third-years got school passes. Then I thought he'd worked for it in the cafe.

"Thanks again." He cleared his throat and nudged Dorian.

"See, that wasn't so hard." Dorian elbowed him back.

Once inside, I parted ways with them, looking for a familiar face. I found Grace and Azrael almost immediately. They were the center of attention because of their costumes, which crossed the line from cosplay over into cinematic quality territory.

"Do you like them?" She grinned and flourished her hands along with the mesh fabric draped between them and the skirts of the black and silver dress. The collar towered over her head, pointed on either side like horns. The neckline plunged to her waist, clearly held in place with dress tape.

"It's amazing, but I don't recognize it."

"Dark Lilli from *Legend*. Az is Jack. I chose them because they sort of rescue each other."

"While saving the world too." Azrael chuckled.

"And wearing lots of glitter." I grinned while peering at his face, which looked practically iridescent. Whatever makeup they'd used matched the finish on the combination plate and scale armor he wore. "How are you going to dance in that?"

"It's pretty light, glamoured to look heavier than it is."

"Let's take it for a spin a little later." Grace jerked a thumb at the stage where Piercing Whispers had finished tuning up. "This dress might not hold up to their first few numbers."

"How about some punch?" Az asked.

"Sure!" Grace grinned. "Thanks." She stood on her tiptoes and kissed him on the cheek, which didn't leave a single mark despite her jet black lipstick.

"That's unsmudgable." I pointed at my lips.

"The new Eternal Glamour line. It's not officially out yet, but I've got connections." She chuckled. "Anyway, let's play that game. Everyone else is ready to go."

"Really?" I blinked.

"It's better to try it when you're off-guard and don't know what everyone's wearing yet."

"Okay." I nodded. "Let's go."

Dylan struck the opening chords of *Doing the Unstuck*, a song they'd practiced at their apartment on my last visit. At least half the crowd hit the dance floor, but not us. Grace led me into a corner, sent a group text, put her phone on record in front of us, and conjured shadows. I knew from experience that her magic would make people fail to notice us, not make us look like a purple blob moving through the crowd. However, we couldn't interact with our surroundings. There wasn't much point in wandering so I stopped Grace, and we stood still. I tried looking for Logan, frustrated. Searching without my eyes was an effort in futility.

It's not, really. Can't you sense him, of all people?

Mind magic worked on line of sight. This search reminded me of wearing headphones on a train. The scenery goes by only generally seen because music is more present in those moments. So I tried thinking like that, attempting to hear and see without ears or eyes. I imagined sensing minds in terms of surface thoughts, vaguely whispered.

That idea might as well have been on the moon.

I'd opened myself to a cacophony nobody else in the room endured. Like being in an electronics store with televisions and radios and music players turned up as high as they'd go except with hundreds of devices, not just forty or fifty. I didn't see the inside of people's heads or hear thoughts. That was telepathy, something only psychics did. Without a device or cooperation, mind magic was vague and sensory, a random collection of humming frequencies. Our textbooks explained that brains have energy, a low-grade electrical impulse, that mind magi could conjure and manipulate.

And banish. The books won't tell you that, though.

I shuddered. At least my inside voice came in loud and clear over that din. Now that I remembered it shouldn't be verbally coherent, the wall of sound began to make more sense. I remembered untangling a box of Bubbe's old costume jewelry, where feeling the knots in silver-plated chains was as important as watching my fingers while undoing them.

Two threads of frequency stood out, off in the corner near the stage. They felt familiar so I walked toward them. A glance at Grace revealed nothing about my guess. Her poker face was on point that night. A pair of costumed superheroes with full-face masks leaned against the wall holding their phones, one in red and black and the other in pink and white, both with spiderweb designs.

I hadn't noticed this anywhere else in the room yet, but something besides the clearly related costumes connected the pair above their hearts, a harmonious frequency that made me think of Beethoven's *Ode to Joy*. And that made it all too obvious.

"It's them."

"Bingo." Grace dropped the umbral magic. "Who are these masked friends?"

"Hal." I pointed at the one in red and black. "And Faith."

"Dammit. I wanted everyone to think I was Miles."

"You're even more heroic, I think. Anyway, she's got more spider-sense than us." Faith pulled hers off too, and they both stepped away from the wall. "Go find the rest. We're hitting the dance floor."

"Just a sec." Hal removed his mask, then tapped the screen on his phone a few times. "Sent it to the group text."

My phone beeped. Grace took me into the corner and activated her magic again. I had to repeat this process three more times. Each would send the video they'd taken of me finding them. Those, along with Grace's recording, would be my proof for the headmaster.

This time, it was easier to sort through, and I found the next pair in a few moments. The thread led me to the bar, toward a knight in wooden armor and a veiled priestess who could have walked off a Tarot card except for the phone in her hand. They had a connection too, loud and clear as the one between Hal and Faith but it made me think of that old Beatles song about friends. I nudged Grace, and she dropped the shadows.

"Hi, Iz. And Lee."

"How did you know it was me?" He lifted the visor on his helmet. "Everyone else from school was clueless."

"Knight of Wands hanging out with the High Priestess?" Izzy winked. When she finished tapping her phone, mine beeped again. "Aliyah's been my divination guinea pig since we were five. Of course, she knows it's us. Let's dance, knight in wooden armor." She grinned at Lee.

"Cool." He nodded. "Are you guys coming?"

"Nah, I've got to find Cadence and Logan."

After they left, Grace hid us again. By then, the wall of sound had reared its indecipherable head again. At first, I couldn't imagine why this exercise had suddenly gotten harder.

This isn't fire or solar magic. Mind is harder to sustain without practice.

I sighed, hoping for a miracle to get through the rest of this strange game. I needed the proof, especially now that I was sure I had mind magic. It came on golden wings.

"Peep?" Ember soared through the air over the dance floor, searching for me.

I'd forgotten she wasn't with me when Grace started this because I always tried to block out her alone time with Gale. Now she wanted to hang out with me. Homing in on the familiar bond was a eureka moment. I tried thinking of Cadence and Logan, picturing their faces in my mind and how I felt with them. I followed the first familiar frequency, trailing it to the door.

I found a pair of women wearing the same green and gold costume, accented with fans. Identical makeup instead of masks hid their faces. One wore her ash brown hair in a bob, but the other's was a wig. That's the one I knew. I didn't hear a bond between them although they laughed together, holding a phone. I nudged Grace, who did the thing with the shadows.

"Cadence!" I chuckled. "Nice *Last Airbender* cosplay! Are you Kenoshi or Suki?"

"Wow!" She blinked. "How did you know it was me? With the wig and everything? Brianna's Kenoshi. I'm too short." Cadence handled her phone, then tucked it away as mine beeped.

"Hi!" Brianna waved.

"What are you doing at the door?"

"Waiting for Piercing Whispers to finish their set because Brelanor is a thing." Cadence sniffed. "Also, Arick's my date."

"No Crow?" Grace blinked.

"Never again." She shook her head.

"I'm sorry." Brianna patted Cadence's shoulder. "What happened?"

"Ask Aliyah." She glanced at Grace's phone, which was still recording. "Or Hal, later. I don't want to talk about it."

Brianna's forehead crinkled. Grace led us away from the door and set up her shadows again.

"One more. How are you holding up?"

"I'm tired, but let's finish this."

Of course, Grace didn't have much more to do. I focused again, expecting difficulty. But it wasn't. Not once I realized that I didn't hear Logan's frequency like I'd done with everyone else's. Instead, it sang in my chest.

"You're humming," Grace said.

"Oh?"

"Yeah. *You're My Best Friend.*"

"I think you're awesome too, Grace."

"No, the song. By Queen."

"Oh!"

Grace dropped the shadows because she had to hurry to keep up with me as I rushed toward a figure in white hooded robes with a pair of wings at the side of the dance floor. He turned while holding his phone in front of him. His head was down, the hood's shadow obscuring his face. I would have known him anywhere, though.

He pushed the hood back, his smile saying more than two year's worth of words. Logan had put something in his hair, making it almost white instead of his usual ashy blond. I knew the character too because we'd watched the Good Omens miniseries over the summer.

"Aziraphale!" I clapped. "Those wings are amazing. You must have put a lot of work into that."

"Not really." He grinned. "I borrowed these from Azrael. That's my favorite of Elsa's dresses, by the way."

"I know." I blushed.

We stood staring at each other. I smiled so much my cheeks ached. Ember sat up on my shoulder, *peeping* at us.

Grace reached out and plucked Logan's phone out of his hands to shut off his camera. Then she did the same with hers. My phone beeped twice in a row.

"You're way too cute." Grace chuckled. "Angel and ice queen."

Azrael sauntered over with cups of punch. He handed them out. "Never would have shipped Elsa and Aziraphale. Aliyah and Logan is another story."

Logan blushed. I gulped down the punch. All that work had made me thirsty. Once I set the cup down on an empty table, he held out his hand. I took it, and we danced through the rest of the Piercing Whispers set. The change between acts took about ten minutes, so we sat. I sent the videos in my messages to my school email to make things easier in the morning.

A man I'd never seen before sat beside me. He wore his black hair shoulder-length and it had ample amounts of silver at the temples. His face was largely unlined. Straight, even teeth smiled from his almost too pale complexion. His eyes didn't twinkle so much as glitter. He wore purple robes adorned with silver chains and skulls. The skeleton mask that went with it rested in his lap.

"Andre Gauthier. Charmed." He put his hand out as if for a handshake.

I focused on the minds in the room again, imagining them as guitar strings and pulling on the most familiar ones. Here was the man Noah wanted to meet, and this was the only way I could think of to call him over without alerting the trustee. If I ended up reeling more of my friends in than originally intended, so be it. I took the adults in charge of Hawthorn Academy seriously and as possible threats. Safety in numbers.

"Um, Aliyah. Morgenstern." I gave him mine, but he kissed it. I noticed he wore black gloves embossed with bones. "Aren't you a trustee for Hawthorn?"

"I know who you are, young lady. Yes, I am." He glad-handed like a salesman. Or a politician. But spookily, in an old "creature feature" way.

"What do you want?" Logan's bluntness surprised me, but I welcomed it.

"Logan Pierce." He grinned again. I realized what he was trying to do. Make everyone he met feel connected to him, somehow. "You were almost my nephew."

"How?" Logan went stony-faced.

"Leo's sister. We were supposed to get married, or didn't you know?"

"Dad never mentioned a sister."

Mr. Gauthier raised an eyebrow at Logan's blank expression. "Never mind that for now. You're both friends with my niece. The good one who takes after me."

Logan and I sat there blinking at him.

"Faith. My sister married her father, unfortunately." He shook his head.

I narrowed my eyes, heeding the inside voice instead of snaring myself in his social maneuvers.

"So you're an undeath magus."

"And you're the extramagus." He grinned again. "Already making a name for herself as something of a hero. We could use more like you."

"She's one of two here." Dylan sat, trapping Andre Gauthier between us. "I'm the other. So, tell me what you've got against Noah Morgenstern."

"Excuse me?" Mr. Gauthier blinked.

"A former student who got expelled last year." I raised my eyebrow. " My brother."

"He got turned through no fault of his own." Dylan pressed his lips into a flat line, and the temperature dropped a few degrees. "You were the swing vote. The one responsible for kicking him out in the first place."

"Ah, well." Mr. Gauthier sighed. "He was an exemplary student and a fine athlete. Talented musically, too. I wish I could have voted otherwise."

"So why?" Dylan asked before the words were out of my mouth.

"Rules. Thurston's arguments were morally correct but procedurally unsound, even if they swayed Dunstable and Glen."

"So change them." The air warmed as I spoke.

"That's...a delicate exercise." He shook his head. "Students whose natures pose a grievous threat to others aren't allowed admission."

"Extramagi are so dangerous that we go on a special registry like vampires." I tried smiling, but it felt more like a grimace. "So I should be expelled."

"And me," Dylan added.

A trio of figures stepped out of the crowd milling beside the dance floor.

"Me too." Dorian lifted his mask. "I came from The Academy. Got a record."

We all blinked. Everyone thought he'd only gone there because his overprotective parents wanted him to live in a fortress.

"Yes, Mr. Spanos." Mr. Gauthier nodded. "You do, but your sentence is over. Stealing an item from black market mobsters is hardly in the spirit of criminality."

"You have to tell us that story yesterday, Dorian." Noah grinned without showing his fangs. "This was all my idea. I only want my diploma, Mr. Gauthier. With you on campus, along with Faith, I don't see how I could be a threat. Please, bring my situation up at the next meeting."

"We don't have one until February."

"That's fine. I only need to study for and take the final exams. I can wait."

"The classrooms aren't sunproof."

"I get accommodations," Logan said. "My IEP says I can take tests in the library if needed, and there aren't windows in there. Why not Noah?"

"You certainly have some dedicated advocates, Mr. Morgenstern." Mr. Gauthier sighed. "I'll bring it up at the appropriate time, but no guarantees."

"Yeah, I know. Some of the trustees aren't so reasonable about vampires." Noah raised an eyebrow at Gauthier's costume. "Thanks for not being one of those."

"You'll each owe me a favor if I succeed."

"No." Noah shook his head. "Only one of us benefits so only one owes—"

"Then I choose Mr. Pierce."

"I ought to owe you." Noah blinked.

"It's okay." Logan nodded. "He says we're practically family."

"Then it's settled."

His phone beeped so he excused himself. The main performer didn't bother introducing himself. Everybody in eastern Massachusetts knew Aurelius Voltaire. He opened with the song *Vampire Club*, which packed the dance floor. I hoped it would give Noah good luck. Logan and I stayed out there for four entire songs.

"Can I cut in?" Dylan asked.

"Yeah, I wanted some water anyway," Logan nodded. "If that's okay with Aliyah?"

"Sure."

Dylan and I danced through the opening of *When You're Evil*. He shook his head, chuckling at the lyrics with a strange smirk.

"What?"

"The irony in this song. I wanted to ask you something. Extramagus stuff I don't want to say on campus."

"Go on."

"Do you, like, see things?" He glanced to his left. "Um, that other people don't see."

"No, can't say I have."

He gulped, hands trembling.

"You're not going crazy." I drew a deep breath. "I hear stuff other people don't. It's something that can happen to us. A way of sensing magic."

"How do you know?"

"Logan's been researching it." I sighed. "The records are super obscure, mostly written by an old green dragon in the sixth century who researched all kinds of rare extrahumans. He tested similarities between dragons and us. Extra magic sense happens to them, too."

"Dragons see colors when there's magic?"

"Colors? Not always, but mostly. Is that why you're such a beast at Bishop's Row now? You see everyone's conjures before they happen?"

"Yeah." He laughed. "It's useful that way. And a total relief to know I'm not losing my marbles. Thanks, Aliyah."

We danced through to the final verse before he spoke again.

"Your mind trick worked, you know."

"Hmm?"

"You called us all over there when Gauthier showed up."

"How'd you know it was magic?"

He pointed at his eye. "You looked like a spider, in the middle of a web."

"What color is it? The mind stuff, I mean."

"Blue. Almost like Professor DeBeer's lightning, but with more green in it."

"You should make a list sometime of all the magic colors. Keep track."

"So should you, with the sound." He chuckled. "Bet it'd make a unique research project at uni someday."

I had nothing positive to say to that, so I kept quiet. Logan returned at the end of the song, and Dylan left with a wave.

At the side of the dance floor, I noticed a flurry of movement. It was Noah, approaching Jonah with his face almost literally lit up. Then joy fled from my brother's face like a hind from a wolf. The reunion soured and he took to the dance floor alone, moving as if to a dirge instead of the spooky yet upbeat music. At first, I almost asked Logan for a break so I could comfort him. Before I could, I realized what was missing.

I hadn't been able to sense it as concretely over the summer, but back then, they still seemed bonded somehow. Like their care for each other was tangible.

Now, there was nothing at all that connected the two of them.

After an entire year nursing a broken heart over his ex Darren, Noah was back at square one. In a brutally ironic contrast, Ember and Gale wheeled overhead, in what every nature show on magical critters would describe as a courtship flight. The pit of my stomach sank along with Noah's, while simultaneous elation lightened my head. All the emotions felt too big for my body, so no wonder they leaked from my eyes.

I sniffled and put my head on Logan's shoulder. He patted my back and murmured in my ear.

"Whatever it is, I'm not going anywhere."

"Thank you." I lifted my head and looked at his face.

Instead of grim determination like the last time he'd said those words, his expression was almost impossibly tender. I heard it now— the song Grace said I'd been absently humming. If it hadn't been for everything we'd been through together, I might have chalked my feelings up to bleed from Ember's courtship. But no.

I'd gone and fallen in love with Logan Pierce. But was he interested in romance? Did I even feel that way, or was it more like Bubbe's relationship with Grandpa? Did big love always have to be cinematic romance?

"Logan?"

"Yeah?"

"Would you mind if... I mean. May I kiss you?"

"Oh!" He blinked. "Nobody's ever asked me that before."

"No?"

"They just did it." He grimaced. "Without asking. Like that's the normal thing to do. So I ran away both times."

"Wish I'd been as smart as you." I patted his back. "Should have kicked Alex in the shin and left."

"You couldn't, though." He sighed. "Doris said you smelled like poison that night."

"I wish I could get a do-over."

"Listen, Elanor didn't always know she was lesbian. She kissed a boy and didn't like it. When she kissed a girl, she called it her second chance at a first kiss." He cleared his throat, then leaned in close. "I want to try kissing you sometime. But not now. It's...too many people here. I'm sorry."

"Don't be. I get it."

We hugged, then kept right on dancing. The silence after the last song nearly startled us. When we looked around, everyone from Hawthorn had left already. Ember glided sleepily down from her perch on the crown molding and settled on my shoulder. We walked out into the night air together, crossed the street, headed up the driveway at 10-1/2 Hawthorne, then through the back gate. Ember took off up the back stairs inside, and that's where we nearly parted ways. Then Logan tugged my sleeve.

"Yes." His eyes shone bright blue in the faint light from the upstairs doorway. "If you still want to, let's try it.

I nodded, unable to think of any words, let alone the right ones. It didn't matter. We got our second chance.

Our first kiss was a little breathless but perfect all the same.

CHAPTER SIX

"I don't generally check email on weekends, but since this is a matter of import beyond the walls of this campus, I shall make an exception."

I sat, waiting as Hiram Hawkins logged in on the computer his son had purchased the summer before my first year. Somehow, he looked out of place using the machine although Bubbe wasn't much younger than him. I'd never felt that way watching her keep medical records. For some reason, he flipped open a folder on his desk although he didn't look at it.

Maybe Mom was right, and Bubbe's generation was all over the place in terms of comfort with technology. Eventually, he stopped clicking and frowning. Sounds from the night before emitted tinnily from built-in speakers, giving me an unsurprising sense of déjà vu. I'd put them together in a playlist, so only brief pauses separated each video. Silence stretched after the last one finished. I didn't dare break it first.

"It seems you do have mind magic Miss Morgenstern."

I only nodded.

"It's as I expected. And rather unfortunate."

"How?" I blinked.

"Any other year, I'd have no choice but to expel you from school."

My mouth dropped open. I couldn't speak, could barely even breathe.

"Mind magic is risky and rife with potential for academic unfairness, accidental or otherwise."

"Aren't there accommodations?"

"Yes. Which is why you may be allowed to finish out the year and obtain your diploma. If you agree to them."

Say nothing.

"Anything."

Oh no.

"You will see a tutor twice per week, as a way to ensure you do not, inadvertently or otherwise, violate the minds of classmates, faculty, and staff. Additionally, Director-General Rockport will fit you with a device that you must wear during all athletic practices and events, lab practicals, and exams taking place on this campus."

"I'm already in counseling twice a week, sir."

"Then you will have extra obligations four days of the week. It's the only way to make things fair."

"That's bullshit, Gramps." Hal Hawkins stepped through the door, followed by Logan and Faith.

"Language, Harold."

He shrugged. "Aliyah's saved lives on this campus. It's unfair to treat her like this."

"I understand all the familiars in this place." Logan crossed his arms over his chest. "Are you making me wear a device in exams too?"

Faith only glared with her hands on her hips.

"The safety of everyone here is my direct responsibility, including Miss Morgenstern's. If I do nothing, she is at risk of persecution, Harold." The headmaster stood. "Even the most intelligent familiar in history can't dictate entire essays during exam periods, Mr. Pierce." He raised an eyebrow at Faith. "Before any of you say another word, this meeting is being officially transcribed."

Faith blinked. Logan paled. Hal's nostrils flared.

"I'm not afraid to go on record." Hal's lip curled. "Tell Aliyah who tutors mind magic before making her agree to this."

"Abraham Fairbanks." The headmaster sighed. "And technically, she verbally agreed before you walked in the room. To anything."

"Then I insist on auditing her lessons, Grandpa." Hal smirked.

"On what grounds?"

"To take notes regarding the family business. trustees aren't supposed to teach except in emergencies. I don't want us stuck without a mind magus on staff when I'm headmaster in the future."

"Future?" The headmaster's eyes widened. "Harold, you—"

"Are you disowning me?"

"No. But magiglobular anemia has no—"

"I've read all the literature." Faith's smile was pure saccharine. "Over fifty percent of patients with magiglobular anemia live through their twenties and over twenty percent into their thirties. Of course, there's no cure yet, but in ten years, who knows? He'll probably outlive you, sir."

Faith's bluffing. His case is more advanced than that. But say nothing.

"I'll allow it." He flipped open a folder on his desk. "But you must designate an alternate to take notes if you are too ill to audit."

"No." Hal shook his head. "If I'm ill, we move the session to the infirmary."

"And if you're in the hospital? What then?"

When Faith opened her mouth, the headmaster held a finger up to silence her.

"You'll be with him, Miss Fairbanks. And we must avoid conflicts of interest between you and your father."

"I'll do it." Logan glanced at Hal.

"Brilliant." Hal beamed. "Who wouldn't want the valedictorian to help out with tutoring?"

"Then we have a plan." The headmaster wrote on the paper inside the folder, then turned it toward me. "You begin on Monday."

I read the paper, which had automatically filled in all of our verbal agreements. He'd signed it, and there was also a space for my name. However, something was missing.

"What about Director-General Rockport, sir? The device?"

"He'll contact you soon. A copy of this exact agreement is on his desk at this moment. Remember, be on your most conscientious behavior while meeting the terms of this agreement. Violating code of conduct while in tutoring sessions may result in probation or even expulsion."

"Okay." I leaned forward, took a pen from the cup beside his name-plate, and signed.

I straightened, then turned my back to follow my friends out of the room. When I had one foot across the threshold, he cleared his throat. I turned.

You forgot to thank him.

"Thank you, Headmaster. I won't forget your advice."

"Same," Hal murmured as he closed the door on his grandfather.

"Well." Faith stooped to scoop Seth into her arms as Ember flew down from the perch across the hall. "How screwed are we?"

"Totally." Logan stared at Doris, who paced ahead of us the entire way out into the lobby.

Once out there, Dylan hurried over to us.

"Did you hear last night?"

"No, what?" I asked.

"I did." Faith sighed. "Tempe's guilty, but I didn't want to say anything. Too angry about it."

"Yeah." Dylan scowled. "Because she barely got a slap on the wrist."

"How?" Logan blinked.

"Wrongful death for bringing that device on campus, because of the professor." Dylan's lip curled up in a sneer. "That's it."

Hal opened his mouth, then shook his head and sat on a bench.

"What about Noah?" My throat felt too tight. "And Mercy?"

"Accidental." Faith kicked at the bench's leg. "They said one mistake shouldn't ruin her life."

"So much BS." I clenched my fists.

"More like so much money. The court fees for wrongful death and the accidents are enormous." Faith narrowed her eyes.

"She's not coming back here, is she?" Logan gulped.

"Nope." Hal looked up. "Expulsion is serious business. It wasn't just ineligibility, like with Noah."

"Dad said he's sending her to The Academy." Faith frowned. "She'll be on the long-term plan. That's when they stay past getting a diploma until the staff thinks they're rehabilitated. Better there than at home, I guess."

"How do we tell Noah?"

"Your brother already knows, Aliyah." Dylan sighed. "He's how I found out."

"Dorian, then?"

"I don't know." His stomach rumbled. "Let's think it through over breakfast."

We got our food but didn't talk any more about it. Later, on my way to the gym to run laps, I saw Dorian leaving the office. He was wiping his face on his sleeve. It'd be better for him to know, but maybe that's why he'd been in the headmaster's office. Perhaps I was too late.

Only one way to find out.

"Hey. Are you okay?"

"Not now, Aliyah." He shook his head. "Sorry. I need to be a wreck in my room."

"The trial?"

He nodded and hurried away without another word. Julia glided after him on silent wings. Later, I saw him in the café, shirtsleeves rolled up to the elbows, scrawling words in a notebook as though if he wrote fast enough, he could outrun the past. I took one step toward him, but Alex gave me a death glare. A hum in my head told me something was different between them, although I wasn't sure what or how.

What would Bubbe do?

I headed to the counter instead. "What?"

"You butt in too much." Alex shook his head. "He needs time and space."

"I believe you." I turned toward the door.

"You're backing off?" He blinked.

"Take good care of him."

"Or else what?"

"Or else nothing. I'll butt out."

"Maybe you shouldn't."

"What was it you said last spring? You owe Dorian your life?" I gave him a tiny grin. "You'll do the right thing for him."

I walked away finally. Once I'd fully turned my back, I smiled as tears welled in my eyes. Maybe this was Bubbe's wisdom proved right, that hurt didn't just come before healing. Sometimes it came in tandem. Maybe something decent could come from last spring's pain and anguish, after all.

The next day before dinner, I had my first tutoring session with Mr. Fairbanks.

"See you later." Logan hugged me. "Do you want me to make a to-go order for you? We're eating in the lounge."

"Yeah, thanks." I pulled back and smiled at him.

"Be careful." Faith studied her fingernails.

"We will." Hal grinned.

"If I had a magic lamp, I'd wish there was some other way." She crossed her arms over her chest. "It's not safe."

"I know," Hal said. "But the buddy system works."

"I'm not sure." Faith looked from him to me. "I hope you're stronger than him."

"Me too." I nodded. "I'm scared."

"That's good." She nodded. "Stay on guard. That goes for both of you."

"I've got insurance." Hal reached into his blazer pocket and scooped Nin out. "She'll literally squeal if something goes sideways."

"It's me." Logan grinned as Hal passed her over. "I'm safer than State Farm."

"*And* he doesn't wear tacky khakis." Dylan peered around the corner. "Or make sales calls at three in the morning."

We all chuckled.

"Come on, Ember." I tried coaxing her down from my shoulder, but she clung on.

"Doesn't she want a playdate with Gale?" Dylan raised an eyebrow.

The moment he spoke that name, my familiar launched into the air and flew in circles, peeping her lungs out.

"Well, there's your answer."

Everybody waved. I took one last look over my shoulder, then walked with Hal down the hall. Unfortunately, this tutoring session was in the same room Ms. Khan used for counseling.

"His tactics are so on the nose that it's almost insulting." Hal snorted, a habit he picked up from Faith.

"Hmm?"

"He wants you to let your guard down, sitting in here." He shook his head.

"Ugh." I rolled my eyes. "If I stay vigilant, I bet he hopes it means counseling's less of a help in the future. So, what do I do?"

"I vote for vigilant. If it's horrible, I play sick, and we're in the infirmary. Faith knows what she's talking about, so there's this, too." He patted the notebook he'd brought.

"What's that?"

"Double insurance." He tilted his head, then pointed at the door. "That's all for now."

He's inside.

I nodded as we crossed the last few feet before walking into the lion's den.

"Sit." Mr. Fairbanks gestured at a metal folding chair in front of the desk. The cozy chair Ms. Khan used sat in a corner.

I did, finding it cold and too slippery. He ignored Hal entirely, as though he wasn't there. So, Hal sat on the couch and put his feet up, shoes and all. He held the notebook on his lap with one hand, smiling as he gave a friendly wave. Mr. Fairbanks didn't even turn his head or glance in his direction. He also said nothing at all for an entire minute. I know because I watched the second hand moving around the clock behind him.

"Um, sir? Is this detention?"

"It's mind magic, Miss Fairbanks." He tapped the side of his head with one finger. "You'll have to show me you'll do it here. Focus. Or I'll tell the headmaster this isn't working. You're aware of the consequences?"

"I'm new at it, though." I blinked. "I mean, the first time it showed itself was in the test."

"I find that hard to believe." He narrowed his eyes.

"It's true, though."

"Prove it."

"How?"

"Either your videos misrepresented your abilities, or you're unwilling to meet the terms of your accommodations. I don't care which it is." He scoffed. "If you can't think of a way on your own, the headmaster will hear of this and will remove you from campus."

I needed help and Hal was only supposed to observe. Stumped, I consulted the inside voice in a desperate attempt to discover the problem.

You closed your mind off to him the night of the masquerade ball when you hid with Dorian and Alex. You're still blocking him.

Shouldn't I be? Faith flat-out said he's dangerous.

Not when it'll get you expelled. He's using this situation to get you out of his way. That's a danger, too.

I tried relaxing, but it was no use. Remembering the fear in my friends, how horrifying Temperance was as his favored child, made that impossible.

"I'll allow you to waste three more minutes of my time."

Don't think about him or the night in question, the voice pleaded. *Find something else.*

"No."

I couldn't, so I didn't. If Abraham Fairbanks, the architect of so much horror, wanted a display, he'd have it. I immersed myself in last year's memories of the locker room, awash in swampy ice-rimed water, blood on Jonah's face, and my brother's neck. The flat, metallic stench of old machinery. A fanatic's crazed glare framed by green and brown hair. I imagined the lighting board in the auditorium, with my hand on the follow-spot, aiming it at his eyes in what I hoped would be an arresting if not blinding display.

Well, you've got his attention now.

His face lit up momentarily. I'm not sure what reaction I expected, but it certainly wasn't what I got.

"Brava." He clapped, one corner of his mouth tilting up. His eyes remained sharp and hard, like a board riddled with rusty nails. "Clumsy, but powerful enough."

I sat blinking, wondering how he wasn't shaken. The memory that still tormented me and a handful of my friends made him feel, what exactly?

Happy. Proud. Vindicated.

"Of what?" I slapped my hand over my mouth as a wave of nausea pressed the remains of my lunch upward.

"To be formidable eventually." He'd misheard me. "Although I doubt you'll ever have the stomach to use mind magic to its fullest potential."

"Thank you, sir." I removed my hand.

"You may go." He waved a hand at the door.

I stood and hauled my satchel up to my shoulder.

"Aren't the sessions supposed to last forty-five minutes, Mr. Fairbanks?" Hal stretched, leaning back more firmly against the couch cushions. "I don't want Grandpa to get the wrong idea."

"Think of this first one as more of an evaluation, Hawkins." He scrawled something on a piece of paper. "The headmaster just got notice of this day's completion, along with my reasoning."

New words appeared on the page, in an untidy copperplate I recognized as Hiram Hawkins' handwriting. Hal rose, sauntered toward the desk, and had a look. He nodded and let me lead us out of the room.

In the lounge, I had almost no appetite but managed to choke down half a turkey sandwich. I fed Ember the rest as she sat in my lap. Nin draped herself around Hal's shoulders like a scarf.

"Let me see." Faith pointed at the notebook Hal had kept in his lap the entire time.

He handed it over, and she flipped through it, nostrils flaring and cheeks reddening.

"What did you show him, Aliyah?"

I told her. Logan held my hand. Dorian hunched over in his seat, pale and trembling. Hailey and Bailey Overton tried walking in the room, but Eston stopped them with a wagging finger. Bailey turned and left while Hailey leaned in the doorway, tugging Kitty's sleeve.

"It's okay."

"It's not." Hal sighed. "Or it won't be unless I do some work tonight and tomorrow. Do you mind if Aliyah and I partner up in lab tomorrow?"

"Knock yourselves out." Dorian looked up as Julia the strix landed on his shoulder, hooting softly. "But why?"

"Don't say anything." Faith shook her head. "Off-campus chatting only."

"That's right." Hal nodded.

"Okay." Dorian sighed. "See you all on Saturday, then."

We gathered up paper napkins and cups and brought them to the trash. Everyone headed upstairs, but Dorian lingered. Before putting my foot on the moving steps to let them carry me away, I looked over my shoulder. He stood, head bowed, leaning between the fluted column and the garbage can beside the lounge's doorway. Alex came with a cart full of bags from other cans around campus. I almost went back until I heard an unmistakable hum coming from their direction.

Alex tapped his knuckles against Dorian's shoulder, then stared at his feet as he spoke.

Dorian nodded and wiped under his eyes with the back of his hand.

Alex shrugged, then pointed at the cart and said something else.

Ice and poison. Like Professor Luciano.

The hum got stronger and more melodic until I knew what would happen almost before I saw it.

Dorian gazed up at Alex, eyes wide. Then he laughed. Fully, from the gut with the sort of smile I hadn't seen since before that horrible night last spring.

Somehow, Dorian Spanos navigated the rocky coast of tragedy, and Alex Onassis was along for the ride. No. They were in the same leaky boat together, taking turns with the paddle.

I got on the moving staircase and said a prayer, hoping it wouldn't strike them again.

On Friday afternoon, Director-General Rockport met me at Bubbe's office. My parents, Noah, Bubbe, and Logan sat in the kitchen with me. An army of classmates along with Izzy and Cadence waited in the backyard with hot cocoa. There wasn't room inside, but they all wanted to support me. Everyone at Hawthorn Academy had gotten a direct link to the video of my extramagus test before it posted on social media across multiple verified accounts. I wasn't sure whether it had gone viral yet.

"This range-limiting unit restricts mind magic. It activates when worn and means you'll be unable to sense or influence other minds unless you maintain physical contact with another individual. You are required to wear it during exams, quizzes, lab practicals, and competitive games. I'd suggest wearing it to practice as well, so you grow accustomed to playing without the use of this particular magic. Do you understand?"

"Yes, I do."

He handed over a small box, the kind gifts of jewelry come in. I half-expected to see a necklace inside, possibly with a locket or something.

"Ears?" I blinked. Because that's what they looked like, except made of pale gold metal instead of flesh.

"Ear cuffs, to be precise. Devices like this must be worn on either side of the head. Now, put them on."

Bubbe held up a mirror so I could see what I was doing. The ear cuffs hooked on the top of my ear and had tiny levers with rounded stoppers at the back to hold them in place. They felt so impossibly light I couldn't imagine how they'd stay on during Bishop's Row without getting crushed.

"Wow." Logan peered in the mirror over my shoulder. "You look like a Sidhe."

He was right. The tips of the cuffs had points and extended far enough above my natural ears to mimic Sidhe anatomy. They almost looked nice but didn't feel that way. The levered clamps pinched, and the metal tingled where it touched my skin. Even worse, they emitted a constant discordant hum nobody else seemed aware of. That made sense, considering my brain interpreted mind magic aurally.

"Are you comfortable?"

"Not really, no."

"In pain?"

"No. It's annoying and pinchy."

"Good."

Dad clenched his jaw so tightly I heard his teeth grind. Mom put her hand on his arm and shook her head. Noah bared his fangs. Ember and Doris both hissed. Logan rested his chin on my shoulder.

She's so brave. My hero.

I blinked. That wasn't the inside voice. It was Logan's. The ear cuffs didn't only decrease the range of mind magic. They seemed to compress it. Maybe I couldn't hear people and the connections between them with these ersatz torture devices on, but the thoughts came in more like telepathy, somehow. Had telepaths had a hand in making these? Was it only because Logan and I had a bond? My eyes stung.

"Are you sure there's no pain?" Rockport asked.

"No. Just my dignity."

"Hmm." His brow furrowed. "I had hoped the aesthetic design would help with that."

"You made them?"

"No." He shook his head. "But I selected them from the vault with you in mind."

"Thanks for that."

Before he could move too far away, I patted his hand.

A wordless wave of guilt and grief crashed around me as if I stood on a storm-swept shore of an ocean made from tears. Staring into the Director-General's eyes, I understood his profound despair. The man might have haunted several of Dylan's nightmares, and even a few of mine, but he was the one drowning. Had he known what this job would entail when he'd taken it? Considering how unprepared I felt for adult life, I thought it likely he didn't.

"I'm sorry, sir."

"Noted." He placed a card with a phone number and email address on the table. "Contact me if there are issues with the device. Are there further questions?"

I shook my head. My family followed suit. Bubbe escorted him out of the kitchen. Nobody spoke until we heard the front door close.

"That son of a bitch."

"Noah!"

"I'm a grown-ass adult, Mom. And he's a government-mandated sadist who's tortured two people I—care about."

"He's not a sadist."

Bubbe froze in the doorway. Everybody did like they'd been encased in ice. A moment later, everyone's voices overlapped.

"—can't possibly know his—"

"—trauma response—"

"—like a robot without feelings—"

"—reputation as a stoic—"

"She touched him," Logan finally said. "He said they work with physical contact. She must have felt something."

"Thanks." I nodded. "That's what happened. He's a wreck on the inside. Guilt, sadness."

"Sorry," Noah snarked. "Not sorry. However he feels about it, that test is evil. Everyone knows about it now. It's been all over the internet for the last two days."

"Did he mention anything about that?" I gulped and glanced at the door. "Before I got here I mean."

"No." Bubbe raised an eyebrow. "But a news brief on a viral memory charm video about extramagi aired this morning. They didn't show the content, but implied it's not a hoax. I can't imagine he hasn't heard."

"I wonder." Dad stroked his beard. "Why did you ask that particular question after you admitted to reading his mind?"

Mom tilted her head, appraising me. "Did you have something to do with this, Aliyah?"

I nodded and cleared my throat, then told them everything.

"That's why your friends are all outside." Bubbe put her hand to her chest. "You don't do anything by halves."

"Well, you're grounded." Mom narrowed her eyes. "Go upstairs and stay there for the weekend."

"Why?"

"You didn't lie when we asked, but you omitted big time. Smuggling a restricted item into a government test. Not asking for help in a dangerous situation."

"She did, though," Logan countered. "She asked me. I did the omission thing too."

"Then you're also grounded." Bubbe shook her head. "I know you're an adult, Logan. But if you're staying here this weekend, those are the rules. Otherwise, campus is the place to be."

"Yes, ma'am." He hung his head and paced out of the room. I followed him down the hall, holding the box the ear cuffs came in.

"Sorry for mixing you up in this."

"Mix happens. I'd do it all again a million times for you." He opened the door to his hidden room. "See you on Sunday?"

"Sunday." I nodded.

Once he closed the door behind him, I headed up the stairs.

"I'll tell your friends they'll see you after the weekend," Noah called from the bottom.

I didn't have the heart to thank him for that until much later.

CHAPTER SEVEN

The whistle blasted so loudly I almost thought Coach Pickman broke it.

"Morgenstern! Front and center!" She pointed at Lee on the bench. "Fill in, Young!"

I jogged over, passing Faith as I left my teammates practicing on the court.

At first, Coach said nothing, which wasn't her usual method of ribbing. She glared directly at my ears as if her scrutiny could deactivate the devices clipped there. I hung my head, ashamed. With good reason. I'd fumbled five saves and missed every fakeout Dylan made.

"Take those off, Morgenstern."

"I'm not allowed to—"

"Practice with them off, I know." She nodded. "But we're off-court for now. You can put them back on in a minute."

I did it, letting the ear cuffs sit in the palm of my right hand.

"Now, look out there at them and tell me what you see."

I faced the court and watched.

"Grace dodged Dylan's ice, but he's following up with air. She's out."

"How long have you had it, do you think?"

"Coach?"

"The," she pointed at her head. "Whatchamacallit. Jedi mind tricks."

"I don't know." I shrugged.

"Seems to me, since before I met you."

"What?" I blinked.

"Morgenstern, your brother I mean, always said you cared too much." She twisted the whistle's lanyard. "He's not wrong, but it's because you pay attention to your teammates and opponents. Until today with those fracking things." She pointed at my hand.

"Wow, Coach. I never thought about it that way."

"Do extra practice off-campus. With alumni and those star players from Messing and Gallows Hills. Collins, Micello and Mendez. Bring Pierce the elder and your brother too."

"Why?"

"The only thing we mitigate in Bishop's Row is damage. The rest is twenty percent talent and sixty percent training. Experience." She wrinkled her nose at the cuffs. "Colleges don't require bull—uh, extreme stuff like those. The scouts are coming this spring. They should see you at your best."

I didn't know what to say to that. Coach must think I had scholarship potential at least.

"Thanks, Coach." I nodded. "I'll talk to my friends in town about practicing, but I'm not sure there's anywhere with space for it."

"I'll make a few calls to Salem State. I've got connections there. Let me know when you have a group together."

"Shouldn't I bring the rest of the team though?" I fastened the ear cuffs on again. "In the interests of being a good captain and all."

"Whoever's able. Don't bother asking Onassis though. He's confined to campus." Before I could ask why, she blew her whistle again and sent me back in, this time calling Dylan back.

Practice went better with me playing reverse point. Or maybe without Dylan and his famous fakeouts on the court. Eventually, we moved on to straight-up throw and block drills, where I partnered with Lee.

"I don't like those." He glanced at my ears, then blocked my solar orb.

"Same here, but they're required for this and tests." I conjured fire this time.

"Hmm." Lee faked right and tossed left. I managed to dodge but not block. "Double standard."

"How?" I threw, obliterating his half-conjured orb.

"A mind magus trustee is walking around without those." Lee brushed ashes off his hands and conjured again. "One with a grudge against you."

"Yeah, but who's going to call him on it?"

"I kind of hoped you would."

"I'm just trying to graduate, Lee." I sighed. "The headmaster says this is the only way to make sure things stay fair for everyone."

"Right." He tossed and tagged my arm. "What if it's unfair to you?"

"This magic just showed up." I reset my ballistae then conjured solar again. "I got by without it for two years here, right?"

"I don't think so." He tossed, tagging me in the middle this time. "If it's not new, then this is all wrong."

The whistle blew, ending practice. I sighed, canceled my conjure, and dropped my hands. I took the ear cuffs off again, finally for the rest of the evening. Izzy always said her favorite thing about Lee was his observant nature. He must have noticed stuff I didn't, as Coach had. I couldn't bring myself to agree with him out loud. In my heart, I knew he had a point.

The guy has an entire harpoon. If Fairbanks knew you had mind magic since Parent's Night in first year, he's exploiting this situation. And you.

I'd never know unless I could literally get a hand on him while wearing the ear cuffs. I didn't want to do that. What I'd seen in Director-General Rockport's head was bad enough. Abe Fairbanks' mind had to be an even worse place. It was probably impossible anyway since the tutoring sessions required me not to wear them.

See? More of a reason to think he's up to something.

"Maybe Rockport gave me a gift."

"Are you okay?" Grace put her hand on my arm.

She said something else about the locker room, but I missed exactly what. That palm against my biceps made Grace's concern feel like the weighted blankets Nurse Smith gave to Temperance's survivors last year. I still had one in my room for the bad nights. My eyes misted over. I shook my head.

"Practicing in that contraption must suck." She tugged my arm. "Let's get cocoa after we clean up. With the tiny marshmallows."

I nodded and went along with my roommate, telling her about the off-campus practice idea as we washed up and changed.

"Sounds awesome." She grinned. "Glad Coach is looking out for you. Because the tournament in spring is off-campus, and you can play in that without the emo faerie jewelry."

In her typical fashion, Grace drifted through the locker room's common area, getting almost everyone else on board for extra practice. Alex avoided her, but I expected that. He was in the café when we got there, alone with his notes from class. He turned his back to us, head down, which surprised me. I got up to put my mug in the dish bin, then lingered by his chair.

"Hey." I shuffled my feet. Ember lifted her head off my shoulder. He looked up when she *peeped* softly.

"What?"

"Sorry you can't come to the extra practices. You're a real asset on the team."

"You don't have to say things like that. Not after what I've done."

"I know, but it's true." I shrugged. "Anyway, maybe you can make it out sometime. Stranger things have happened, right?"

"No." He glanced at the doorway behind me. "I haven't been off campus since I got here from Greece, remember?"

"Right." I nodded. "Anyway, good job at practice."

I made the thumbs-up gesture at him before walking back toward Grace, who was getting ready to leave. Sure enough, Mrs. Onassis stood near the doorway, talking to her familiar. She spoke loudly and distinctly enough for me to hear every word.

"Every poison has a remedy, doesn't it, my pet? Even the ones that act on the mind. Some work slowly, but they're still effective."

Once we got into our room and were ready for bed, Grace asked the million-dollar question.

"Was that trustee threatening you?"

"I don't think I want to know."

"This is starting to feel like a case of same vulture, different liver."

"I'm no Prometheus, Grace."

"Could have fooled me, Aliyah Morgenstern. Fire, light, big ideas. You always bring it. And buzzards like her keep showing up."

"I give in. Here are my chains." I shook the box with my ear cuffs inside before I set it on my dresser and shuffled toward my bed. "Now I need Heracles to break them."

"Hmm." She yawned. "Soon, I hope. Goodnight, Aliyah."

"Goodnight, Grace."

I closed the blue book and set my pencil down on top of it a minute after Faith, fifteen after Hal, and twenty behind Logan. We sat, glancing at each other as we waited for Dylan and Dorian. The ear cuffs buzzed, which was pretty much the only difference between this day and the last time I'd taken a test. So, the dampening device didn't affect me here as much as it did on the court.

The inside voice didn't chime in about this. Had it spoken up any time I wore the cuffs? No, not that I could remember. Whether it came from mind magic or not, I had no clue. The only information I had about it was what Professor Luciano had said, that he thought it came with being an extramagus, an idea that Dylan's auras supported. We hadn't found anything further, no matter how many books Logan borrowed on interlibrary loan.

"Excellent." Professor Hawkins clapped his hands. "You've all finished ahead of the time allotted. Take a break in Creatives, and I'll see you all for the Lab practical after lunch."

"A round of applause for you, Prof." Dorian applauded back at our teacher, moving his hands in a circle. "This is the best I've felt after a test. Thanks!"

The professor cleared his throat a few times as he went around the room to collect the blue books. A tiny grin played at his lips, and I figured he held back laughter that might have been considered inappropriate. But why?

I turned my head. Mr. Pierce stood in the back of the room by the door with Brand the phoenix on a perch over his head. Both the magus and his familiar wore grim expressions, as though they'd watched a battle to the death instead of teenagers taking a test where everyone finished early and cheered the teacher.

After collecting my things, I stood. Dylan, Dorian, Faith, and Hal were already headed for the door. Logan still sat in his seat, his hand hovering over his pencil as though frozen in time. I strode across the row toward him.

"Come on, let's paint." I picked the pencil up and put it in his hand, making sure not to touch him. He knew the ear cuffs made me sense thoughts and I wanted to give him privacy.

"Um, yeah." He swallowed, then nodded. His shoulders shook but not with cold.

"What's wrong?"

"I can't say it." Logan stood, keeping his back to his father. He slung his backpack on as though it could stop him from shaking. He inhaled, then with a slow and deliberate motion, took my hand. I saw way too much. Including the first time Logan almost died.

The childhood memory flashed between my mind and his in an instant, but its events had helped shape his life since then. Of that I was sure, even if the circumstances were still a reeling blur from my perspective. It'd take time to sort through and piece them together. One thing was clear. Leo Pierce was every bit as horrible as Abe Fairbanks.

Professor Hawkins's voice connected me back to the present. I wasn't sure what he'd said but knew what I had to do.

"We're getting out." I squeezed Logan's hand. Although he still trembled, he nodded.

The entire way through the room and the doorway, he ignored his father and only had eyes for me.

"I'm sorry," he said while sitting in front of a blank canvas.

"Hmm?"

"The, um, hatching." He stared at the still-empty palette in his hand. "It was awful."

"You never spoke of it. If you ever do, I'm here."

"It's easier to express stuff like that without words." He nodded at the canvas. "But scary. Because once you put something on canvas, there's your life for everyone to judge. Even the people who wanted it kept secret."

"Hey." Dylan sat nearby with his guitar. "An awesome guy once told me if your art's amazing, it needs to be heard. Or seen, in your case. Your life is yours to depict. If people don't like their part in it, oh well. They should have treated you better."

"Aliyah?"

"He's right." I handed him the tubes of black and white paint. "Why not do a portrait of that giant cat hero?"

Dylan raised an eyebrow. When neither of us responded, he shrugged and strummed chords. Logan's eyes lit up, and he put paint on the palette, then went to work. I finally removed the ear cuffs and stashed them in the box in my blazer. Then I stayed near the door, watching in case Mr. Pierce tried to audit us in here. He stayed away the entire time.

We had an auditor for the Lab practical too, but it was Andre Gauthier. He kept quiet for the most part, his owl asleep on his shoulder. Their presence didn't disturb any of us. Unlike with the lecture final, the ear cuffs made everything harder for me.

We moved around the room individually, taking turns at the benches. They were set up as numbered stations each with an item we'd all seen before during the semester. And no instructions. We had to remember what to do with each of them. I'd studied, but trying to recall my notes only produced a faint buzz as I gazed at the watch glass and dropper bottle. Out of time, I moved to the next station and let Dorian take my place. I shook my head at the graduated cylinder and foiled metal.

Usually, the inside voice would have chimed in by now, at the very least to tell me I was an idiot. But it didn't. The ear cuffs had to be blocking it out. So I tried to imagine what it'd say.

"Do something," I mumbled.

"Shh." Professor Hawkins put his finger over his lips.

Right. Silence was mandatory. I reached out and picked up the cylinder. Then I remembered. We infused the metal before pouring the solution on it. If my mind wasn't working, at least it seemed I could get results with muscle memory. Or magic memory or whatever. I managed to get back to the station that stumped me before the end and do something with it.

My revelation didn't mean I aced the practical. My grade came back as a B minus, lower than usual for Lab. The professor called me to his office before dinner, which is why I knew about it before folks started leaving for break.

"What happened, Aliyah? You've been in the top three for practicals every other time." He cleared his throat. "I'm not the greatest instructor for magipsych lab, so if there are methods I didn't use that help you, please let me know."

"It's not you." I rummaged in my bag and produced the ear cuff box. "It's these."

"Ah." He shook his head. "I'll do some research over break and look for study methods you can try."

"You don't have to, Professor. It's probably a matter of practice. Bishop's Row was harder when I wore them, too. Since I put them on in gym every time, I'm adapting. I should have worn them in Lab every time, too."

"I don't like that idea." He sighed. "I'll look into it anyway if you don't mind. It's better to have more than one plan."

"I just didn't want you to go out of your way, is all."

"It's the least I can do."

I nodded.

As I headed out of his office, I noticed a photograph hanging on the wall. It was Professor Luciano, sitting at the desk that now belonged to Professor Hawkins. A wall of melancholy sound washed against my back, like a wave breaking while wading out of the ocean.

Guilt, shame, grief. Of course. What will you do about it?

"Thanks, Professor." I opened the door. "I can tell you care about all of us."

With that, the tide of his negativity receded.

Faith's parents had already left for Rhode Island to move Temperance into The Academy.

"They said they don't care what I do with myself." She watched the teaspoon make a whirlpool in her morning coffee. "Guess I can finally live the dream of getting pregnant and dropping out."

Hal had a coughing fit. Lee put a hand over his mouth. Dylan's mouth dropped open. Logan's face went beet red. Alex ran his coffee cart into a table.

"Come to wassail at the Ambersmith's," Grace said. "Az asked me to invite everyone. So all of you should. It's on Twelfth Night, which is January fifth." She looked over her shoulder at Alex. "It's a blast."

"Bollocks," Dylan said. "I'll be back from NYC by then, but Piercing Whispers has a gig that night."

"Aww." Grace pouted. "What about the rest of you?"

"I haven't been since grade school. So excited!" I clapped my hands.

"What's wassail?" Logan asked.

"It's where Christmas caroling comes from," Dylan said.

"In January?" Lee blinked.

"They do Yule caroling too, in town," Grace said. "On Twelfth Night, they sing to the trees at their orchards in Danvers first, before coming into town. And there's tons of hot cider."

"I'll try it." Logan nodded.

"What do you think, Hal?" Faith gripped his hand.

"I want you to go even if I can't, Faith. Make videos." He nodded. "I think it'll be ready in time, so you'll probably see me for the in-town part."

"What?" Dorian blinked.

"It's a surprise." Logan smiled. "You'll find out in a few weeks."

"Not me. I'm going home." Dorian glanced at Alex. "Maybe you'll send me a postcard, Xan."

"I can't."

"The post office is down the street."

"No. I mean I can't leave campus to mail it."

"Hmm." Grace stirred her coffee. "You know some people, just saying."

"No." Alex shook his head. "No magical sneaking hijinks. I'm only allowed to walk Dorian to the train. Or else."

Nobody knew what to say to that. After a moment, he remembered the cart and pushed it back through the cafeteria to finish his work.

I went upstairs to pack, and Logan to fetch his already prepared bags. We made it down to the lobby, where everyone else in third year waited. The familiars huddled together in a cuddle pile on a bench, all aware of what came next—a brief parting of ways for many of us.

Kitty was heading out to Portland, where she had a college interview. Eston would meet her before New Year's after seeing his great-grandmother in New Hampshire. Hailey and Bailey would leave the next morning on a train to New York City, traveling at the same time as Dylan and his mom, who'd go sightseeing and take in a Broadway show. Lee was staying at the Mendez's. Grace would visit the Amber-smith's extended family in Haverhill. Only Hal and Faith would remain on campus.

We turned on Washington Street toward the train station. The temperature was cold enough to nip our noses although the puddles still splashed in response to several sets of booted feet. I watched Alex and Dorian walk together, hands down between them but not touching.

"Are you sure you don't need me to stick around?" Logan asked. "To finish the project, I mean. My parents have shows in Vegas through New Year's so that's not stopping me."

"If so, I'll get a message out." Hal grinned. "I think we've got it."

Hal and Faith said goodbye at the top of the stairs. He looked worse than worn out, dim somehow, although not unkempt. Faith gave him her arm as they walked away. The rest of us descended behind Alex and Dorian.

"Slow down. You're not on the track." Grace elbowed me. "I think they want a little space."

"Oh, sorry." I hung back. "Are they—"

"Dating?" She raised an eyebrow. "No. I asked yesterday."

"Uh, that wasn't what I meant."

"What then?"

"Are they okay? They both look weighed down."

"I don't know."

At the bottom of the stairs, I jogged to catch up with them. Dylan and Grace bolted after me. Even Logan tried to keep up. Up on the platform, I realized I'd caught them mid-argument.

"So fight back." Dorian's eyes reminded me of icicles in March, almost liquid.

"You don't understand. I can't. Like, I freeze up." He shook his head, mouth a thin flat line.

"I totally get it. Cowardly ice man here, remember? You can do this. I believe in you."

"Maybe I shouldn't." He glanced at Grace and me, Logan and Dylan. "Maybe I deserve what I'm getting, after what I've done."

"Or what you've always gotten from her is the reason you screwed up." Grace crossed her arms over her chest. "Going against the grain is hard, but it's important."

"I don't know your story, DuBois." Alex sighed. "Probably should have asked instead of writing you off. Sorry."

"Hey, that's a step." She nodded. "Keep going."

"I'm trying, but she pulls me back every time."

Dorian put a hand on his shoulder.

The train squealed to a halt, brakes and engine hissing out plumes of steam. We waited it out and said goodbye. Dorian stopped in the doorway.

"Get on, Xan." He held out his hand.

"What?"

"I've got enough cash to get you a ticket on board. Come with me."

"I've got nothing with me. No clothes."

"I have three entire closets."

"But your parents—"

"Always ask when I'll bring friends over, already."

"She'll think I ran away." He hung his head.

"Run toward a welcome, then." Dorian smiled.

He stood, hands opening and closing, shoulders trembling.

"Go. It worked for me."

Alex looked at Logan like he'd just walked out of the Under.

The conductor called for all passengers to board.

Dorian stepped sideways, making room in the doorway, and beckoned.

And just like that, Alex Onassis escaped for the holidays.

CHAPTER EIGHT

Only Hope For Me
Logan

The morning of the Ambersmith's annual wassail, I sat up, still awash in the worst of my nightmares. Doris headbutted my side, then went behind me and leaped up to my shoulder where she perched, purring in my ear. She always knew when it was worst and never left me alone in those times. I sobbed, head in my hands, because of how lucky I felt to have found her.

"Was it him again?" I heard in her purr. "On the mountain?"

I nodded, then told her the entire story for what had to be the thousandth time.

No decent parent puts small children in a territorial animal's nest. My father wasn't decent in any way. He was a stunning performer and a brilliant marketer, an iron-fisted trainer, and a demanding instructor. Decency only got in the way of talent, he said.

He barked orders at us from a much safer position, yards away, with a rock wall to his back as we sat in a feather-bedecked circle beside a clutch of ash-smeared eggs the size of my head. He expected both Elanor and me to bond with the phoenixes that were about to hatch right there in the nest. She'd used fire several months earlier, but my magic hadn't even come in yet.

When my sister picked up one of the eggs, it blazed. The one I tried stayed cool under my hand. Nothing happened after touching two more, so Father shooed me away. I followed his orders as obediently as the animals he commanded. Because I'd been able to understand them ages before I started talking, which was later than normal. I knew what happened behind the scenes, things my parents never mentioned. Not long after that, I saw it firsthand. So, I started back toward him, shuffling my clumsy feet over loose rocks and sloping terrain. I fell on my backside in stone and scree when something cracked behind me.

Elanor's eyes went wide as the shell burst into a million flaming pieces. Father ordered her to banish every one, but she wasn't strong enough. The nest she sat in caught fire and my big sister cowered in fear, clutching a tiny featherless and ashen hatchling in her arms. That's when it happened. My water came in like a tidal wave, although I'd never seen the ocean. It doused the entire nest. I cried because I might have harmed the eggs to save Elanor.

She hurried out of the nest and ran toward me. I tried to follow although my feet never moved well without a beat to guide them. Father grabbed me by the shoulders and shook me so hard my head snapped back and forth. He lifted me, too. Held me in the air at the side of that treacherous drop.

"That wasn't even the worst part, Doris."

She rubbed her head against my cheek, absorbing my tears into her glossy silver coat.

"It's what he said afterward." She meowed.

"Yeah." My voice hardened, imitating his. "Give me one reason not to toss you like garbage, retard."

Back on the mountain, I couldn't get a word out. Both the baby phoenix and Elanor shrieked at the top of their lungs, almost matching in volume and pitch. I understood the bird better than my sister. Both cried out for help.

It came on velveted paws.

An enormous black and white feline, larger than a tiger but not one on account of its scaled hindquarters, leaped down from the ridge above us. It roared, startling my father back from the edge.

I shook, unable to conclude the story because sometimes the dream had me landing on solid ground as it actually happened, sprawled with Elanor, watching our father flee.

In the dream last night, I went over the side, screaming at the rocks below as the mysterious hybrid cat-dragon tried in vain to catch me.

Doris didn't press again. I mumbled words of love and thanks while scratching behind her left ear where she always seemed to itch.

"We should go upstairs for breakfast soon," I muttered although my stomach felt like a washing machine. "And yeah, I'll wash up first."

The spare room had a tiny bathroom, with a shower I thankfully fit in. Once I was decent, I opened the door that separated my room at Bubbe's from the animals on the other side. Finally, I smiled at the din of their combined voices, comforting in a way that a room full of people talking wasn't. People mystified me, for the most part. They pushed in too much with their voices and bodies. It was different with magical creatures. I could listen to them all day long, stand in crowds of them for hours.

Nobody in my family, not even Elanor, understood that about me. I'd tried explaining, maybe a hundred times. That I felt out of place almost constantly, homesick while sitting at home. Until I wound up here, where the critters came for healing.

Bubbe got it. She couldn't hear them as I could, but she'd devoted her life to their care. Even the ones actively dying.

No wonder Aliyah wanted to be like her. I did too, which is why I paced up and down the hall, stopping at each Dutch door to say good morning to all the patients and boarders. I found Aliyah's grandmother in the room closest to the waiting room entrance, checking on a karkinos, her underside berried with a clutch of eggs. They weren't exactly like a regular crab's. Instead of thousands, the eggs numbered only ten. The mothers carried the baby crabs on their backs after hatching, too.

"I can't wait to see your children, waving with their little claws."

The mother karkinos clacked in response, saying it'd be a relief to have the weight on her back for a change.

"Good morning, Logan." Bubbe grinned.

"Hi, Bubbe." I smiled back while looking at the crustacean instead of her, which she'd never complained about. "Are you coming upstairs for breakfast?"

"In a while." Which meant she wasn't.

"Can I bring anything down for you?"

"You're so thoughtful, Logan. Some toast and marmalade if they've any to spare. Thank you."

"See you later." I waved at them both.

Every morning since I started staying here, she always gave me a kind word. The first two weeks, I'd been a wreck over it that she'd go out of her way to drop a compliment. I discovered it wasn't extra, only how the Morgensterns did things. Still awkward, but way better than my family's exacting demands.

Upstairs it was the same. Aliyah and her parents passed words of love and gratitude along with dishes of food, like sentiment was something sweet to sprinkle over life in general. I sat at the table, giving and receiving in the space they made for me. If only it could be like this forever. Someday, I'd have to move on even if I'd left Las Vegas for good. College. Extraveterinary school. Those places might be more like home than here. That scared me, almost enough to make me give up on my dream.

Then Aliyah smiled at me.

I grinned back and blinked. Not because her expression surprised me. All her smiles were like sunrises. Different every time but beautiful. Other guys at school called Aliyah Morgenstern pretty, and they had a point. That kind of thing wasn't important to me, though. The best thing about her was her heart. It was like the ocean, vast and powerful, a force of nature. She cared. Noah said too much, but there's no such thing. Caring is like oxygen. Everyone needs it, and it's a catalyst that lets amazing things happen.

By the time I remembered them, my eggs and toast were cold. Mr.

Morgenstern put my plate in the oven, which he always kept warm during breakfast.

"It's too easy for some of us to get distracted," he explained. He'd been talking about Aliyah's mom, but that habit he got into for her helped me too.

"Speaking of distraction." Aliyah rinsed her plate in the sink. "I totally forgot yesterday to mention it. That book we ordered on inter-library loan came in. We should go to campus and have a look."

"Right." I nodded. "That's the book we can't take off-campus. Maybe you don't want to spend half the day in the library."

"We're going out tonight. Plenty of excitement there." She put the plate in the dishwasher, then dried her hands. "I'm game if you are. Besides, who doesn't want to read the musings of medieval dragons?"

"Hmm. Probably Bailey Overton. She always says dragons are so last week."

Although she'd proved me wrong for over two years, I winced, expecting a reprimand for answering a question I only realized was rhetorical after the fact. But she smiled at me, followed up by a hug this time. I hugged back. Over her shoulder, I had a perfect view of her parents, framed by the doorway into the living room. Their rela-tionship looked like a classic romance; something Aliyah probably wanted in her life someday.

Although we'd kissed three more times after the masquerade ball, the way I felt about her hadn't gotten any different. There wasn't a rush of blood away from the head like Eston described when he and Kitty had alone time. I didn't get all tingly like Hal said happened with him and Faith. I was comfortable with her, pleasantly warm like being under a blanket on an autumn afternoon before the heat kicked in. Or like the swimming pool at the penthouse in Vegas, bathwater temper-ature. That's the way it was since the first Parent's Night. Something everyone else I knew described as platonic.

I loved her more than I ever thought possible, but like almost everything else about me, the way I loved wasn't how everybody else did it.

Aliyah deserved a conversation about that, but we had to go to the library first. I headed out the door she held for me and started down the stairs.

"You need some shoes, Logan. Oh, and we need to grab Bubbe's toast and marmalade."

"Oh yeah, forgot." I chuckled, then went back up.

"Are you sure?" Aliyah gestured at the lexicon. "It's such a pain to translate those."

"It might be painful, but I've got my routine for it." I patted the cover. "I'll handle good old Ludovico's journals while you get our drinks. I mean, it's not like I've got to duel an actual green dragon or something."

"There's no way I'd leave you in actual danger, Logan." She planted a kiss on the top of my head. "You know that, right?"

I nodded. She headed out to get tea, which the Ashfords allowed in their library over breaks and exam weeks. Moments later, I got lost in a puzzle of Old Germanic. Languages were a special interest for me, and I'd discovered that dragon shifters also were by extension because most of them were polyglots, like the dragonets.

Most people wouldn't have realized that, but since I understood magical creatures, I had. Each species had its articulate way of communicating, along with a sort of common parlance conveyed physically. The entire idea of studying, possibly even classifying and recording these languages, fascinated me. So did each of Ludovico's tomes. However, we'd only been able to check them out one at a time from the Black Forest University library, and it took weeks to ship them over.

I went *tharn* to the rest of the world while translating. *Tharn* was an awesome word, as in awe-inspiring for real. I'd always imagined Richard Adams, the man who wrote *Watership Down*, was an extrahuman with an ability like mine, and that he'd chronicled the folklore and history of actual rabbits. Or maybe even moon hares. That made sense with all the Frith and Inle stories anyway.

Usually when I waxed oblivious in here like that, Aliyah kept watch. She said it was to make sure I didn't get interrupted, but it probably had something to do with my dad and his cruel friends. Fortunately, they didn't show up that day. Instead, someone else did.

"That's some heavy reading, young sir." The voice was low but musical, sort of sing-song. It reminded me of my old kindergarten teacher. I felt so comfortable listening to it that I didn't feel the need to look up.

"Uh, yeah. But it's pretty amazing." I didn't look up, merely pointed at the phrase I'd just translated. "Ludovico the Green was obsessed with extramagi. I don't blame him. He found out they have extra abilities, not only their elements. This part mentions dragonets. Did you know they almost went extinct during the Reveal? Ludovico thinks they're significant to extramagi. I haven't finished translating yet, but it looks super interesting."

"I suppose it's hard to compete with unearthing ancient history." A deep beige hand with rounded pearly fingernails set a much newer book beside the Old Germanic lexicon. "However, you should have a look through this. It's no less significant although much more recent."

I only intended to glance at the glossy cover, but the photo of a young woman with a mercat on the cover hooked me. I read the words above and below it.

"It's a yearbook. From Hawthorn. In my Dad's first year?"

"Take care, young sir. I'm not as benign as I seem."

Doris pressed her head against my hand. "No more questions. She's Fae."

Now I looked up. The woman reminded me of someone. I wasn't sure who. Forgetting faces was a weakness of mine, so maybe I'd seen her before. One look at her clothing told me no. She wore a robe. Not the kind people put on before and after a bath or even ones folks graduate in. A caftan. It was long and deep mauve with yellow paisley print. Mirrors decorated the neckline, sleeves, and hem. Grace would have gone nuts over this woman's clothes because they looked both vintage and magical.

"Do you not know who this is?" One of those rounded fingernails underlined the picture.

I shook my head, then turned back to my translation work.

"Do yourself a favor and check the yearbook out before you leave."

All of a sudden, it was too much. Her unexpected presence. The interruption. The mirrors flashing on her sleeves. Was she even allowed on campus? What if she worked for my father? She'd said right out that she wasn't what she seemed.

"You know, I didn't get your name." I looked up. Her face wasn't as young as I'd originally thought, forehead and the bridge of her nose etched with lines. Not the kind that came from smiling, either.

"Mila."

"There's aren't any Milas on the staff here."

"There were, once upon a time." She caressed the cover of the book, then pulled her hand away.

My mind parsed all the possibilities in an instant. She couldn't be a ghost. They couldn't come on campus and without a medium present, couldn't move books. And Doris said she was Fae. She didn't belong here, and adult guests weren't allowed without a legal or blood rela- tion to a student. The Hawkins family saw to that with their space magic. So, there were only two possibilities.

Mila was related to a student. One currently present on campus. Or she was the djinn Aliyah and I had been looking for all semester. If the second was true, so was the first. Could Mila be short for Gamila, as in Haddad-Hawkins, maker of the stained glass mural? I couldn't ask because she was a full-fledged faerie and I'd naively asked her two questions already. I'd end up owing her a favor. I had to do something to get more of a clue. Or maybe let on that I wasn't entirely clueless.

The library's door opened.

"Please, I'm out of time. The yearbook is important."

"I wish I could take your word for it."

She flinched, confirming my theory. I turned my head, looking for Aliyah, hoping she could make sense of Mila's sudden presence. Instead, it was Faith walking toward me, not her.

"I'm making Aliyah take a lunch break, with solid food. You too, so come on." She stuck a scrap of paper in the lexicon, then pulled the ribbon over Ludovico's journal.

"Wait, I was talking to—"

When I looked up, my visitor had gone. My stomach rumbled like it was the underside of a thunderhead.

I went along with Faith and checked the old yearbook out of the library on the way.

Lunch was chicken nuggets with applesauce and mashed potatoes. Childish, people say. Comfort food, actually. Texture and flavor always as expected, without surprises. No matter where or how those three foods get prepared, they're universal. Like Swedish meatballs, but easier to find. I'd already had enough excitement for the morning and a new experience planned for later on. The last thing I wanted was an embarrassing stimming episode, like the night of my birthday. Or worse, a meltdown.

My friends cared. Hal did the right thing always, and I trusted Faith with my life. Those two were fierce and fair, and wouldn't ever hurt me on purpose. Grace went out of her way to include me, even when I couldn't keep up. They didn't understand all of it though. Not like Aliyah. That's why I pretended not to notice Grace's nudge and Faith's raised eyebrow. And why I answered Hal with a little white lie.

"You deserve a better lunch than that, Logan. Want me to ask Penelope what else she's got?"

"Translation fried my brain. It's all I could think of." I gestured at my plate. "Anyway, I'm almost full. Thanks for asking, though."

"So, Grace. Why aren't you at Azrael's?" Aliyah sipped chicken soup from a mug.

"Brought you all something." She grinned.

"Clothes." Hal grinned at Faith. "I bet anyone a cookie." He pointed at the last chocolate chip on the dessert plate.

"Sorry, Hal." Grace shrugged. "Textiles, but not technically garments."

I looked up, my jaw dropping with my eureka moment.

"Blankets!"

Grace pushed the plate toward me. I shook my head at the spoils. Hal shrugged, then gave the cookie to Faith, who broke it into pieces and shared it around to the familiars.

Nin fiddled with her hunk of cookie, trying to get Hal's attention. She had a point. Hal had thinned out a little during his summer growth spurt, but he hadn't ever looked this gaunt. I could see his cheekbones, and his temples had hollows. I crossed my fingers under the table, hoping it was five-o'clock shadow and a recent haircut. He'd started shaving this summer, too. Maybe it was good old rising testosterone and not magiglobular anemia trying to kill him.

Lune turned his nose up at it, insisting he was strictly vegan, then dropped it at Aliyah's feet. Seth and Doris gave their pieces to Ember.

"I wonder why he did that." Faith shook her head. "He never turns down a treat."

I blinked and stood, hearing the animals chatter.

"You guys, she's expecting!"

"No way!" Grace put her hands on her cheeks. "Did you know, Aliyah?"

"Um, well, I knew she'd mated. During exam week." She blushed.

Grace dropped me a wink. Now it was my turn to blush because I understood on an intellectual level what she thought. A familiar's emotions carried over through their bonds. It wasn't uncommon for magi with familiars to get amorous at the same time as a mating familiar. However, I knew for sure that wasn't the case with Aliyah because I'd been with her every night of exam week and we hadn't done anything but typical cuddling. Mostly, she'd been exhausted. Then there was me.

"I'm asexual."

I slapped one hand over my mouth and the other on the table. I was suddenly in my worst nightmare. The one where I *did* end up falling off that cliff in Tibet. My friends all sat staring in silence that stretched like Nevada afternoon shadows until one of them cleared her throat and broke it.

"What, like a sea sponge?"

"Grace!" Instead of rolling her eyes, Faith widened them. "Uncool. It's an orientation, like being bi or gay."

"Sorry." She hung her head. "I know. I meant it as a joke. It didn't come out right."

"Well, neither did I." I sighed.

"Hey, are you okay?"

There Aliyah Morgenstern went again. Caring about the aftermath of my inevitable blurt instead of however she must feel about it.

"Well, that depends. I mean, are you?" I looked up at the shallow bowl of her perpetual slight smile, unable to meet her eyes. "I understand if you want to stop dating."

"That's our cue, I think." Hal wobbled a little as he rose from his seat.

"No, you can stay." Aliyah put her other hand out. "I'm fine, Logan. Relieved." She drew a big breath. "Pretty sure I am too. Asexual, I mean."

I sat blinking at her, breathless. Was this happening right now, in the cafeteria? Coming out to my friends after keeping it secret for a whole year why it hadn't worked out with Dorian? Had I truly gotten entangled with a person who felt the same way I did? My father said that I'd spend my life settling because water wasn't flashy enough to be more than an opening act. Because I was too picky. Because I didn't ogle women or men. Because I was different. Which meant unlovable.

Doctor Morgenstern and her family, especially Aliyah, proved every day that those hadn't been facts, only my father's opinions. Here was more. All my friends sat quietly, giving me time to respond. Although I was slow with this, they didn't seem to mind. Aliyah took my hand. I looked up into her eyes for the few breaths I could manage. I had no idea what to say to her but opened my mouth anyway.

"Thanks for coming out with me." I squeezed her hand. She let go, then held her arms out. I nodded, and we hugged.

Everybody laughed, even the familiars. But with me, not at.

Lunch was over after that. Hal and Faith went back upstairs.

Aliyah and I promised to bring the blankets to them after finishing up in the library. Grace left campus. I put my bag over my shoulder, remembering why it was heavy—the yearbook. I'd missed the chance to talk to everyone about it. But not Aliyah. I filled her in on our way back down the hall.

"I agree." She nodded. "You saw Gamila Haddad-Hawkins. Which is pretty amazing."

"I feel bad though. Don't really have time to look into that yearbook with all the translating."

"I'll do it."

After we sat, I handed it over to her. Aliyah didn't even open the cover.

"This girl could have been a supermodel. She looks almost exactly like you."

"I don't see it." I winced. "Sorry."

"That's okay. I'll figure this out."

She pulled a notebook out of her knapsack and started flipping through glossy pages. I stuck to my alternately pulpy and oily ones. The lexicon was my bargain bin purchase from Wicked Good Books on Essex Street. The interlibrary loan copies of Ludovico's journals were so old they were on genuine parchment.

At some point, Aliyah put the pen down and sat back in her seat. I kept on working. We only had until the Ashfords closed the library and the stuff I'd discovered was essential. The old green dragon had started experimenting with blood. His methods were far from modern in a scientific sense but the magical methods tracked with much of common practice today. I'd be showing all of it to Bubbe as soon as possible.

"I'm sorry Mr. Pierce, Miss Morgenstern." Mr. Ashford bowed his head at each of us in turn, steely blue hair brushing both sides of his cheeks. "That's all the time for today."

I packed up my lexicon and notes, then headed toward the desk to hand the journal to Mrs. Ashford, who checked it back in. When I got back to the table, Aliyah had opened the yearbook to the page showing the name, quote, and plans of the young woman from the cover. Her name was Petra, but Aliyah's finger blocked her last name.

"I know what it says here, Mr. Ashford. What happened to her? Because I know for a fact she's not who this yearbook says she'd be."

"Sadly, it's not my story to tell. Perhaps Mr. Gauthier would take such liberties. Or Mr. Pierce."

I shuddered, fighting the urge to turn and leave.

"I've tried the former. The latter, I don't trust." Aliyah's lips twisted into the grin she always put on before a big Bishop's Row game. Her game face. The mask of defiance. "I'll find a way. Thanks, Mr. Ashford."

On the way out, we stopped in the Creatives room, where the lights were out. They didn't come on, so Aliyah conjured some. Grace's blankets were inside the textiles cabinet on the far wall. After retrieving them, we started toward the doors again. I reached to open them, but she stopped me. A moment later, I heard voices—my father's.

"Frankly, you should have done a better job controlling your son."

"Says the man whose offspring haven't been home in over a year." The woman snorted. I didn't recognize her voice. "You will help me find him. Or I'm spilling the beans on your little plan."

"I'm not sure how a fire magus can help in a missing persons case. Why not call the police?"

"You think I haven't tried? You know how public servants are since the Reveal chaos died down. All about doing the same for everyone, not treating families like ours with proper respect."

"You have a point, Lavinia. So what do you want from me?"

So, the woman was Alex's mother.

"Money, of course. To hire a private investigator. All of mine's tied up in trust at the moment. The holidays, you know."

"This month's dividend already gone?" He chuckled. "You're like a sailor on shore leave with money. How do I trust you to repay?"

"Oh, I promise you'll get paid back. And then some."

Doris and Ember wondered together how asking a friend for help could sound so sinister. They didn't know my father.

"How much?"

She dropped a figure she could have purchased a yacht with. He laughed, and they negotiated. My stomach churned. Finally, they wrapped it up.

"So in exchange for this sum, you will say nothing."

"About what, exactly?" She tittered.

"The conservatorship I've got drawn up. Or the plan we've got to thwart Gauthier and give me grounds to invoke it on him."

"As soon as the funds hit my account, I promise to stay mum on the matter of entrapping your son."

"I'm surprised you're not making a similar demand."

"Oh, Leo." She clicked her tongue. "Nobody likes my son. They don't care how I treat him, not after the things he's done. I understand the need with yours. He's surprisingly popular."

"Like the idiot mascot of the bleeding hearts." My father laughed. Doris hissed. "Elanor's fault entirely. I should have separated them after that incident in Tibet."

"You know what they say about hindsight."

Their voices got smaller, which meant they headed down the hall. I sat. Had to, or I would have fallen. And it would have been a disaster, clattering chairs and them barging in here.

Doris jumped into my lap. Ember, although she'd clung to Aliyah like a statically charged sweater since getting pregnant, draped herself over my shoulders. Trails of smoke curled up to my right. Doris put her paws on my shoulders, purring in my face. When Aliyah sat on the edge of the table beside me and smoothed my hair, it was all over. My self-control.

Tears rained down on my face, sudden and torrential as a thunderstorm but silent as the snow. I'd learned over the years, not just how to cry noiselessly, but how to sob without sound.

I'm not sure how long it went on. Thunder-boomer length, or hurricane? Was this the eye? Would an hour of peace pass, only to blow apart in the next storm surge?

"Sorry," I finally managed and wiped my eyes on my sleeves. It almost felt like a lost cause, but at least my nose wasn't running.

"No." She shook her head. "If Bubbe were here, what would she say?"

"Be quiet?" I glanced at the door.

"No, they're gone." She tapped her temple. "Mind magic says so. She'd say don't apologize for healing."

"Can't argue with Bubbe." I sighed and leaned my head against her side. "Guess it's going to take time. Should be used to that by now."

"Someday, you'll be free from this." She put her arm around my shoulders. "From them."

"How do you do it?"

"Hmm?"

"Be so. I don't know. Unsurprised? That my parents aren't like yours? Because yours shocked me."

"First year was when I started understanding. Nobody's got it the same at home as anyone else. It started with Grace."

"How?"

"I guess you don't know. In first year, Grace told me her parents had passed. Years ago. It hit her hard, and the only thing I could do was be there for her, without judging."

"So, it's like a bedside manner? Something I could learn maybe?"

"Wow." She got off the table and crouched in front of me. "Logan, you don't have to be blunder-free. Making mistakes won't stop your friends from caring."

"Okay." I stood and held my hand out. "I'm ready to go now."

We walked arm-in-arm through the hallway and into the lobby. Fortunately, Faith was there, so we handed the blankets off to her. While separating them off the bundle, we noticed one each for Izzy and Lee, which we delivered to her house. After that, we helped out in Bubbe's office before dinner. I left my translation notes on Ludovico's blood research with her before leaving for the evening.

We met the others in front of the Essex Street municipal parking lot, where we waited until Azrael showed up in a minivan with Grace. At first, I wondered what we'd do about Hal's wheelchair.

That's a misnomer because Hal's prototype didn't have wheels at all. It hovered instead, powered by fans underneath, like a hovercraft. But the fans were magipsychic. Dylan and I helped enchant those, and Lee helped make the frame as lightweight as possible with his wood magic. It was an enormous secret, and Hal couldn't handle all the walking and singing without it.

There was no way Grace or Az could have known we'd need a bigger vehicle. But he held his phone up and tapped something on it. Then he put the emergency lights on, and they got out.

"Do you want the good news or the bad news first?" he asked Aliyah.

"The good." She grinned.

"Bar's coming. He can fit Hal's contraption in his truck. And he's bringing Cadence."

"Okay, what's the bad news?"

"He's got Mavis coming too."

"How's that bad?" She scratched her head.

"She's a Merlini." He sighed. "You know how they are."

"Hold on there." Hal blinked. "Because it sounds like you're pushing bias on a middle school kid."

"It's more complicated than that." Tires crunched on the pavement. A door slammed.

"Complicated or not, she helped us out big time."

"The entire family's horrible."

Everybody stared at him, even Grace. Az shuffled his feet, face turning red. The pit of my stomach dropped. If Azrael felt this way about Mavis over her family, what did he think of me? I shivered. Aliyah put her arm around me. I looked up.

Bartholomew Micello kept right on approaching, but Cadence stopped walking toward us in mid-step. I'd never seen the dark-haired girl whose arm she held, but she looked sad, like a kid with no cake or presents on her birthday.

"We don't do the sins of the father thing here." Hal took Faith's hand. Right. Her family was awful too. "Everybody gets a chance."

"Okay then." Azrael nodded. He strode over toward Cadence and the girl. His entire manner changed like he'd stepped on stage, suddenly in character. "Miss Mavis Merlini, I do humbly apologize for my unkindness. I'm only a changeling, but I owe you one favor in exchange for my uncouth outburst."

"Um, okay?" She tugged Cadence's sleeve. "Like, now?"

"Any time." The mermaid nodded. "But it's simpler to call faerie favors in sooner rather than later. You don't want to forget that kind of debt."

"Okay then." Mavis grinned. "Azrael Ambersmith, I want you to hop on one leg and bark like a dog. Then we're square."

He looked ridiculous but didn't seem to mind acting so clownish. Grace clapped her hands once he finished, starting everyone else off. After the applause died down, we helped Hal into the minivan while Bar put his magic chair in the back of the truck. Mavis jumped up after and strapped it down with bungee cords. Then we were on our way to start the evening's festivities at the Ambersmith family apple orchards across the border in Danvers.

I kind of hoped wassailing would be like musical theatre. But it wasn't. No dancing at all, only singing, which I'm no good at. And lots of hot beverages, which made up for that. The adults had whiskey in theirs, except for Old Grandpa Ambersmith. Along the way, he walked with the younger crowd, regaling us with stories about the adult Ambersmiths. He spoke with a slight whistle, due to missing his front teeth. And he made epic dad jokes.

"My medication goes with booze like ugly Christmas sweaters and the Fourth of July." He dropped me a wink. "Get it?"

"Yeah." I chuckled. "Good one, sir."

"Call me Old Grandpa. Or OGP if you want, kiddo."

"Thanks, I will."

"You've got fine manners, for a Pierce." He elbowed Aliyah. "I approve."

"Oh, um, thanks OGP."

"Like he's a Morgenstern already. When's the wedding? You could double up with Az and Miss Gracie." He glanced at Hal and Faith. "Make it a triple, even."

Aliyah and Faith both blushed while Hal hid his face behind his blanket. Cadence smiled but sighed. Mavis rolled her eyes.

"OGP!" Azrael shook his finger at his grandfather. "Enough with the wedding talk, already."

"This is his usual schtick now, you know?" Grace rolled her eyes. "Time for some new jokes, Old Grandpa."

"Watch out for Miss Gracie. She'll rule the world someday." OGP nodded.

"Nah." She shrugged. "I only want to decorate it."

Everybody laughed.

Somewhere on the north end of Salem, near the bridge to Beverly, I overheard Aliyah and Cadence.

"Why hasn't it been in the papers, though?"

"Does that really matter? I mean, the video's internet famous."

"It was for about five minutes. Mostly, it got me in trouble with my parents. It's yesterday's news now. I thought you said your mom would want to interview me, Cadence."

"Now that I think of it, she hasn't mentioned you or the test video at all. That's strange for her. She's not the sort of adult who's oblivious to internet trends."

"Can you ask her, then?"

"It's tricky, but I'll try."

"Do you need help?"

"Nah. I'll ask her out for mother-daughter mimosas after I get home. I should know something before we go back to school."

"Yearbook." I nudged Aliyah.

"Oh, right!" She nodded. "Cadence, have you ever heard of Gamila Haddad-Hawkins?"

"Hal's grandmother? She's a djinn, works for the Sidhe Queen. She's lamp-bound. Typical djinn story—separated from her family for years because of the lamp."

"How does that work, exactly? The lamp thing?"

"They do three terms of service, for the first three people who acti-vate the lamp. After that, they're bound to service forever unless someone willingly takes their place."

"Another djinn?"

"Preferred but not required. But they've got to be extrahuman and not a shifter. I don't know much else." She shrugged.

"Okay, more library time then." She nodded. "One more name to drop if that's okay?"

"Hit me up."

"Petra Pierce."

My mouth dropped open. So, the yearbook girl was my relative.

"Logan, she's your aunt. That sister Andre mentioned, remember?"

I couldn't speak, so I shook my head.

"Well, no wonder. It's a sad story." Cadence didn't know my father. "She graduated Hawthorn, top of her class. Went to Provi-dence Paranormal for a semester and got engaged to her high school sweetheart. And then there was an accident. Her familiar passed and she got sick. Mental illness, like paranoia and halluci-nations."

"What happened after that?" My voice cracked.

"Nobody knows. Her fiancé never married. Or dated anyone else either."

"I bet you five bucks I know his name." Aliyah sighed.

"Oh?" Cadence blinked. "Go on. I love easy money."

"Andre Gauthier."

"And, I'm broke." Cadence opened her handbag and paid her debt. "I think that's enough gossip for now. I'll talk to Mom tomorrow morning about the other thing."

On the way home, most of us were sleepy. I had my head on Aliyah's shoulder, struggling not to nod off.

"Will I see you tomorrow?" Aliyah asked. I almost told her of course when Hal answered.

"I think so." He hung his head. "After all the court business with Dad pushing Mom out of my medical care, I feel bad going over his head. They'll be angry."

"They'll be angrier if they find out this could have helped." Faith sighed. "Their issues aren't your fault."

"Yeah, I know. But I have to make sure they'll be okay, that I'm not burning bridges with Mom and Dad. I won't have time to fix it later."

I didn't know what decision about tomorrow Hal had to make, but I had too much experience walking on eggshells. So I sat up.

"Hal, it's not your job to fix your parents." I studied his face, half-lit from the orange streetlights outside. "You're trying to survive. Do that however you have to. They're the adults. If they have problems with whatever you're doing, that's on them."

Az turned on Washington Street, and we rode a few blocks in silence. Finally, Hal nodded.

"Okay, so I'll see you tomorrow."

We said goodnight and trudged back to our homes, temporary and otherwise. I kissed Aliyah goodnight at the bottom of the back stairs. Bubbe waved from her kitchen as I passed by, taking pictures of my notebook with her phone. Coming to live here the year before had seemed like my last resort at the time. The Morgensterns were my lifeline now. And Aliyah herself, nothing short of hope.

That night, the dream of the cliffs didn't visit me, and I slept in peace.

CHAPTER NINE

Aliyah

At sunset the day after the wassail, I helped Bubbe in her kitchen, setting two tea trays up on the table. I knew why even before she poured a bag of blood into the yellow teapot decorated with copperplate letter Bs. She put it on a hotplate with a digital display instead of the stove and set it for 98.5 degrees Fahrenheit.

"Is Noah coming over?"

"No, but our guests are both vampires." Bubbe put our usual teakettle on. "They want to talk to Hal about his magiglobular anemia."

"Why am I here, then?" Dylan pulled his head and the carton of cream out of the refrigerator. "And Aliyah?"

"That's extramagus business."

"Can you explain?" My hands shook, and the china rattled. Up on top of the refrigerator, Ember peeped, and Gale chirped.

"Even I'm not clear on the details. They assured me it's positive."

I tried to relax after that. Optimism faded once Hal arrived, hands clenched in tension and forehead twisted with strain. He left his chair in the waiting room and shuffled toward Bubbe's kitchen propped up between Faith and the wall. Once seated, he refused all offers of refreshments. I didn't press about why. After all the effort to get in here, the last thing he'd want was needing the bathroom in the middle of this meeting.

Faith paced the room while Hal sat. Dylan opened a cabinet and brought down tea bags. The table only seated four, so I got a few extra chairs from an empty exam room. I set one each at the head and foot of the table, then glanced around, trying to figure out where the odd one ought to go.

"I'll take that one." Dylan reached for it. "Be a wallflower." He placed it between the doorway and the corner, then sat.

"Hey." Logan paused in the open doorway and nodded at us. "A car just pulled up in the driveway. Wanted to let you know."

"You coming in?" Hal asked.

"I'm about to have my hands full with baby karkinos feeding time. Good luck!" He grinned.

"Thanks."

The door chime sounded, and Bubbe left the room. She returned in moments, leading a man and a woman. The only similarities between them were their pallor and a sense that each was out of time somehow. His clothes reminded me of old movies Bubbe watched. She wore a lab coat over full skirts and a shirtwaist that could have come out of a history textbook about the Industrial Revolution, but her briefcase was decidedly twenty-first century. They sat across from Hal and Faith after Bubbe took the seat at the head of the table. I stood at the foot, leaning my hands on the back of the chair. From there, I had a view of everyone in the room, the door, and even the little window over the sink.

Why are you in defense mode?

"Please, Aliyah. Sit," Bubbe requested. "It's only polite."

"No, I understand." The man grinned. "Your granddaughter has a sense of tactics. Detective Klein, Newport Police Department."

"And I'm Doctor Klein, Director of Magical Conditions at Rhode Island Hospital." She cleared her throat. "Which is part of the reason we're here, Harold."

"My blood tests." Hal nodded. "Call me Hal. Are you related?"

"We were married, once upon a time. That's part of why we asked to meet in person instead of doing this over the phone." Doctor Klein pulled a folder from the briefcase. "With magical anemia cases, my lab also runs DNA profiles. Harold, you share a significant match with both of us."

"What?"

"We're your maternal grandparents."

Hal sat with that for a minute while pouring hot water over a sachet of chamomile. He stirred the tea he never ended up drinking, possibly a picture of calm to the Kleins, who had only just met him. The rest of us knew better. The tea was busywork for his hands. Hal's serious business had gone dire. His next words confirmed it.

"Shouldn't my mother be here, then?"

"I invited her," Bubbe admitted. "She never answered or returned my calls."

"So you knew, Bubbe."

"We asked Doctor Morgenstern to let us give you this news in person." Detective Klein gazed at Hal, his eyes filled with that same light of determination my friend often displayed. "Among other things."

"Okay." Hal nodded. "I'll hear you out."

"When Steph—" Detective Klein shook his head. "When your mother went missing, we never stopped looking. Police in other jurisdictions wouldn't talk to me once they checked my status in the registry. Vampire problems. We hired a psychic investigator, but it led to another young woman instead. Eventually, we realized law enforcement wasn't working."

"So, you went with science." The corners of Hal's mouth turned up. "Medical records."

"Exactly." Doctor Klein flipped the folder open. "It took a long time for older records to go digital. Even then, your mother must have avoided conventional doctors. Dhampyr blood isn't easy to hide."

"That's why I was born on the Hawthorn campus." Hal's mouth

dropped open. "But why? If you loved her so much, cared enough to search for decades. Why did she hide from you?"

"That's a question even we can't answer." Detective Klein sighed.

"She should be here then." His jaw tightened. "She'll hear from me. Even if I have to send Detective Ambersmith to her door again."

"Again?" Doctor Klein blinked.

Hal shook his head, hands balled into fists. Faith put an arm around him. She looked up at me, eyes narrow and nostrils flared. The silence stretched until I broke it for them.

"She managed all his health care, medical records. He had to sneak in here and get a blood test from my grandmother, just to get diagnosed."

"This was the anonymous test from twenty months ago?" Doctor Klein consulted her folder. "That's the first you knew of your condition?"

Hal looked up, eyes shining with tears, nodding.

"No." Detective Klein looked smaller somehow after that. Like he'd deflated. "We're too late."

"Too late?" Dylan blinked. "For what?"

"A license, of course." Faith clicked her tongue. "To turn him before—"

"Before I die." Hal swallowed. "If there's any chance at all, I'll fill them out with you today."

"There's not." Bubbe sighed. "The waitlist is two years long, even for emergencies. I checked right after they called."

"We thought we had more time." Doctor Klein shook her head.

"What about testing his blood?" I straightened. "Get a better idea of how far his progression is? Maybe he's got more time than you think."

"That's a good idea Miss Morgenstern, but unlikely. If he'd known, started those experimental infusions before the onset of symptoms, we'd have better odds. Still, I'll do the tests."

"A long shot's still a shot," Faith said. "Hal's a fighter."

"Not like you." Hal grinned at her. "But thanks. So, what's the other reason you're here? You talked like there was more than one."

"He's got your curiosity, Cal." Doctor Klein flipped through the papers in her folder. "My department's doing research on testing. Collecting samples from as many extrahuman types as possible. We've only got one extramagus in the bank so far and wanted to ask Miss Morgenstern and Mr. Khan if they're willing to participate."

"Is it for magic in the blood, or DNA, or maybe metabolism? Blood only, or cheek cells too? Oh! What about stem cells from teeth?"

"You must have big college plans, Miss Morgenstern." Doctor Klein raised an eyebrow. "To answer your question, we're developing a blood test to identify genetic conditions like Hal's. We're also blood typing for extrahuman ability. We're already there with common shifters and halfway with changelings, but we haven't got enough data from magi. Especially extramagi. And there's a growing demand for an alternative test, considering the news this autumn."

"My grounding lasted longer than that video's had its fifteen minutes." I sighed.

"On television, perhaps." She tilted her head. "In medicine, it's big news. A psychiatric colleague of mine is very interested. She thinks we must abolish the old way of testing. There's a path forward if my test works, but I need a bigger control group of known extramagi. Something more recent than Mr. Pierce's translations. Your grandmother's been sharing those with us and they've been a help in research, but not when it comes to registry regulations."

"Okay." I nodded.

"Sure," Dylan said.

"Have you checked with Nurse Smith at Hawthorn Academy?" Bubbe asked. "Perhaps the infirmary has a sample on file for Filberto Luciano. If you accept a hair sample, I've got some of my brother's. He was an extramagus too."

Hal, Dylan, and I went about the business of donating blood. Faith called Hawthorn's infirmary while Bubbe headed to the basement to get the box of Great Uncle Noah's things. After that, the Kleins exchanged contact information with Hal, who insisted on including Faith. We all waited around as the vampire guests left. Once they were out the door, Hal drooped, unable to rise from his seat.

In the end, Dylan carried him out to the waiting room and placed him in his magical moving chair. Logan, all finished with the now sleepy crab family, listened to Faith relate what had happened as we all bundled up for the walk back to Hawthorn campus. Frigid air pinched at my nose and cheeks. Logan and I didn't linger at the door. We had to meet Cadence down at The Point in five minutes, so there wasn't even time for coffee.

I set a brisk pace, trying to keep warm. Ember helped, snuggled inside my coat like a hot water bottle with scales. Logan carried Doris the same way. He struggled to keep up by the time we got to Harbor Street, so I slowed. Cadence beckoned to us halfway down the block from the apartment building she lived in with her parents, turning down a side street I recognized.

"Is she taking us to Noah's?" Logan asked.

"Looks like it."

Sure enough, Cadence lingered by the basement entrance. A hat and scarves covered her entire head and most of her face, not a typical look for her even in the depths of winter. Once we reached her side, she rang the bell on the door's frame.

"So, what's—"

"Shh. Inside."

I stood in the cold, blinking. The last word I'd use to describe Cadence was covert. Somehow, that's how she acted. Elanor let us in, and we all walked past her down the stairs, letting her follow us down.

Instead of sitting on the futon or one of the beanbags in the living room, my friend headed straight into the soundproofed music studio. Once we were all inside, Elanor closed the door behind us and remained outside.

"Okay, what gives, Cadence?"

"You guys, this is serious." She tossed her coat on a stool, unwound the scarf, and removed the hat, revealing red-rimmed eyes, tear-blotched cheeks, and half her hair shaved off.

"What happened?" Logan gasped. "You look like—"

"2008 Britney, I know."

"No, not her." Logan blushed. "Cyndi Lauper."

"He's right. It's more of an undercut."

"Hmm. You two don't lie about stuff like that." She sighed. "I feel more like Britney all the same."

"What did Crow do this time?" The room warmed up a little too rapidly. I drew a deep breath and banished the tiny flames around my hands.

"No, Aliyah. It's about last night." She sniffled. "My mom. She's not who I thought she was."

"What?" I blinked.

"Not her, not Dad. Not me either." Cadence wrung her hands. "Our whole family, we're not ambassadors. We're exiles. So, Mom has no strings left to pull. She's got to stay in her lane at work. Or she's out of a job, and we're out on the street."

"That's horrible!" I ran to her side and put my arms around her. "Cadence, I'm so sorry."

She cried on my shoulder for a while. I wasn't sure how long, but Logan came over and patted us both on the shoulder, holding a box of tissues. Although in other ways Cadence wasn't acting like herself, in her sadness, she remained the same friend I'd always known. Mercurial and thoughtful.

She pulled back, wiping her eyes on her sleeves.

"Triton's Beard, Aliyah. Don't apologize. It's not your fault."

"It's mine." Logan held a small globe of water and stared into it. Doris rubbed against his legs.

"No." She sniffled again. "That's not how it works."

"Wait, what's happening here?" I blinked.

"Sorry for borrowing your tears, Cadence. Water never forgets." Logan spoke at the globe. "How did I not see it before? How much did my father pay them?"

"Too little." Cadence's voice shook. "Even if it had been billions, too little."

"Probably it was a threat." He sniffled. "That's more his speed."

"What did he buy?" My voice sounded tiny, squeaky. Cadence opened her mouth to answer three times but couldn't manage.

"A kraken egg." Tears streamed down Logan's face. "He wanted me to bond with her, but she never even hatched."

"Kraken are sacred to merfolk." Cadence choked back a sob. "So, the DelMars are exiles. Forever. Down the entire family line. And we're not supposed to tell outsiders why. Or swim past the shallows."

We ended up in a hug pile on the floor in the middle of the room. Eventually, someone knocked on the door. I got up to open it and found Elanor and Izzy on the other side with more tissues and mugs of hot cocoa. Cadence and Logan walked out shortly after I did and we each took turns washing our faces in the bathroom before joining our other friends in the living room.

Cadence told them about the exile situation, how the reason was a secret. Elanor flat out accepted the fact that she'd never hear it, but Izzy drew some cards before nodding and letting it go. After we'd all calmed down, I asked the question that had been bothering me the entire time.

"Why not come to my house for this?"

"To be honest, I think all of you ought to find somewhere else to meet off-campus. Because the Morgenstern house isn't safe." Elanor sighed. "It's connected to the school, and our dad and his cronies are nothing nice."

"We can't invade your space all the time. You guys need to practice if you want to pay the rent."

"What about the extra Bishop's Row practices?" Elanor nodded. "Salem State's gym is safe enough, and I'm there if you want help."

"Oh yeah." I winced. "I was supposed to put a group together but dropped the ball."

"Dylan ran with it, so you're good." She grinned. "He asked Noah, Bar, and Brianna already. So Izzy, how about it? Extra Bishop's Row practices on Saturday mornings? Just until the week before the tourney."

"I'm in." She sighed. "Maybe one or two more teammates can make it but most have other obligations on weekends."

"I'd better captain better." My laugh came out all nervous. "Sorry."

"Can we do cheer stuff too?" Cadence jerked a thumb at Logan. "I hadn't considered extra training."

"Sure, why not?"

Noah walked through the door, hung his coat and a green apron on the coat rack, and went to change. Dylan and Arick showed up a few minutes later because Piercing Whispers had practice.

The rest of us stuck around to listen in and help them decide their next gig's setlist. Before she left, Cadence thanked everyone for helping salvage the evening.

The story continues with book nine, *True Dedication,* coming soon to Amazon and Kindle Unlimited

GLOSSARY

- **Changeling**- A mortal child of either one or two faerie parents. Most changelings choose a monarch sometime in their twenties, although some do it earlier than they have to.
- **Dampyr**- The mortal offspring of two vampires. They aren't as rare as many suspect, although because their blood is exceptionally sustaining to vampires, they keep their status secret. Dampyr sometimes have magic or psychic powers that work unreliably.
- **Faerie**- A term used to describe either a changeling who has tithed to a monarch and spent a year and a day in the Under or the pure creatures such as Gnomes and Pixies who were created by the king and queen.
- **Ghost**- A dead person with unfinished business becomes a ghost. If a mortal makes a contract before death, that gives them unfinished business and lets them linger. When ghosts finish their business, they move on, but no one knows where they go from here.
- **Magus**- A mortal who can use magic. Magic comes from

energy in the world. Most magi can only use one type of magic. However, a rare few can do more than one kind. Those are called extramagi.

- **Merfolk**- People who can live on land with legs or in the sea with fins and tails. They only emerged from the ocean after the Big Reveal and are still extremely rare outside of harbor towns.
- **Psychic**- A mortal with psychic power. Psychic ability comes from a person's own body and mind.
- **Vampire**- An unliving person who drinks blood to survive and enhance their abilities. Only regular mortals, psychics, and magi can get turned into vampires. Shifters, changelings, and faeries won't turn, and most of those won't survive an attempt.
- **Shifter**- A mortal who can take an animal's shape. Shifters have one form, with coloring similar to what they have while human. They usually have an enhanced sense while human-shaped, which goes along with their animal. For example, an owl shifter might have keen eyesight and a wolf shifter, a great sense of smell.

Shifter Varieties

- **Dragon**- The only shifters who can see both magic and psychic abilities, though only while shifted. The most powerful ones can partially shapeshift. Dragons are immortal and reproduce infrequently. There are so few of them since the Reveal that they've started taking other magical shifters as mates.
- **Kelpie**- A magical shifter who gets their abilities from an enchanted faerie pelt that bonds with their soul. The Kelpie pelts were created by the Goblin King, so they have Unseelie energy and restrictions. A Kelpie's animal form is a horse. Families pass the pelts down through generations,

and part of each ancestor lives on to help their descendants. The ancestors can get distracting, however.

- **Selkie**- A magical shifter who gets their abilities from an enchanted faerie pelt that bonds with their soul. The Selkie pelts were created by the Sidhe queen, so they have Seelie energy and restrictions. A Selkie's animal form is a seal or sometimes a sea otter. They can use water magic as long as they wear the pelt. Families pass the pelts down through the generations, and part of each ancestor lives on to help their descendants. The ancestors can get distracting, however.
- **Tanuki**- A magical shifter with enhanced speed and the ability to see all types of magic while shifted. They are also the only creatures who can manipulate luck, causing it to turn from good to bad or the other way around. They stop aging if they own a charm infused with luck from humans. Very few of those charms exist, having been either used up during the Reveal or locked away.

Powers

- **Air magic**- The power to conjure, control, and banish wind or air.
- **Earth magic**- The power to conjure, control, and banish earth, sand, or rock.
- **Empathy**- A psychic power to sense and influence emotions in other people.
- **Fire magic**- The power to conjure, control, and banish flames.
- **Ice magic**- The power to conjure, control, and banish ice.
- **Lightning magic**- The power to conjure, control, and banish lightning.
- **Poison magic**- The power to conjure, control, and banish poison. Each magus has a slightly different type of toxin they produce. Some are even antidotes to others.
- **Precognitive**- A psychic power to foretell future events.

- **Spectral magic**- the power to conjure, control, and banish light.
- **Spectral Affinity**- A trait some spectral magi have that makes them charismatic and believable.
- **Summoner**- A psychic power that lets the user make contracts with pure faeries, letting the summoner call them in times of need. Each creature has an anchor, some item symbolizing the bond. Mastery of summoning takes decades of study, which is why the most powerful are either vampires or past middle age.
- **Seelie**- The Sidhe queen's court. The Seelie way is about following the letter of the law, even when it's hard or cruel. They have a hard time reconciling faerie rules with the new mortal laws since the Big Reveal.
- **Solar Magic**- The power to conjure, control, or banish sunlight. Some of the most powerful practitioners can find hidden objects or discover long-kept secrets.
- **Solar Affinity**- A trait some solar magi have that makes them beacons for coincidence.
- **Space magic**- The power to move the self or objects instantly across distances. Some can even move other people.
- **Space Affinity**- This space power comes with an ability to locate people or things important to the magus.
- **Telekinesis**- A psychic power that moves objects.
- **Telepathy**- A psychic power to read minds.
- **Tithe**- The process of pledging to either the queen or king, making a changeling choose to be either Seelie or Unseelie.
- **Umbral magic**- The power to conjure, control, and banish shadows and veil or camouflage objects or people.
- **Umbral Affinity**- A trait some umbral magi have that makes them difficult to remember without psychic ability, faerie magic, or a shifter pack bond.
- **Undeath magic**- The power to conjure, control, and banish unliving energy.

- **Unseelie**- The Goblin king's court. The Unseelies bend the rules and often navigate mortal society more easily than their Seelie counterparts.
- **Water magic**- The power to conjure, banish, and control water.
- **Wood magic**- The power to conjure, banish, and control wood. It takes extreme power to influencing a living plant.

Creatures

- **Basilisk**- A venomous serpent that also has poison magic.
- **Dragonet**- A tiny dragon-like creature, always associated with one or more element which powers their breath attacks later in life. They have scales but are warm-blooded like birds. Most don't get much bigger than a small cat.
- **Familiar**- A magical or mythical creature who makes a bond with a magus.
- **Gryphon**- A chimera which has the head of a bird and hindquarters of a predatory mammal. They come in several combinations of base species, and habitat influences their choice in magi to bond with.
- **Karkus**- A crab that can change its shape. They're said to be the offspring of the crab that pinched Hercules as he battled the Hydra.
- **Lightning Bird**- A familiar from South Africa with an affinity for lightning. Its beak can jump-start a car.
- **Mercat**- A shapeshifting feline with fur for land and scales in the water. They can live in lakes, rivers, or in the sea as well as on land. They must never completely dry out, or they will die.
- **Moon Hare**- A magical rabbit that gets power from its particular moon phase. They commonly bond with umbral magi.
- **Pharaoh's Rat**- These natural predators of dragon shifters are the size of ferrets and resemble a mongoose with more

fur. They have an affinity for space magic and can use it on occasion.

- **Pigeon**- Not as mundane as most think, some pigeons have an uncanny sense of direction due to their affinity for air magic.
- **Pricus**- An aquatic goat said to be descended from Capricorn. They can warp time even better than Gnomes.
- **Pure Faeries**- Creatures who spring to life from magical sources in the Under. They are genderless, and their type and ability depend on place of origin. They're associated with only one court, although they will work together to defeat a common enemy.
- **Sand Cat**- A feline that lives in the desert, able to go for weeks without water. Earth magic lets them do this.
- **Sha**- A magical desert dog from Egypt. Sha are the size of mundane toy breeds with short hair and small pointy ears. They could pass for mundane except for their blue tongues. They are attracted to anything undead.
- **Sphinx**- A magic cat with an affinity for fire. The reason they're hairless is that they're resistant to flames.
- **Strix**- A venomous owl with an affinity for poison. Female striges have rounded tufts on their heads, while males have pointed ones.
- **Sumxu**- A lop-eared cat found only in northern China. They are masters of camouflage and have an affinity for several kinds of magic.

Places

- **The Academy**—Something between a community college and a military academy for extrahumans, the Academy is geared toward helping extrahumans who don't play well with mortals get ready to join a blended society. It's got divisions for learners of all ages, though they are housed separately.

- **Cherry Blossom School**- A dojo geared toward teaching extrahumans self-restraint, meditation, and how to temper their enhanced physical abilities with more mundane skills. It's been around for close to a hundred years, run by the Ichiro family. Mundane classes used to be offered as a front but now are a separate division.
- **Ellicot City Magitechnic**- A prep school for magi and psychics specializing in magipsychic technology. It's located outside Baltimore.
- **Gallows Hill School**- Traditionally for shifters, this prep school in Salem recently opened its doors to changelings and other extrahumans not categorized as magi or psychics.
- **Hawthorn Academy**- A preparatory school for magi in Salem. Its campus is in the space between the mortal realm and the Under, giving it unrivaled privacy. They specialize in teaching familiar magic.
- **Providence Paranormal College**- A school founded just one year after Brown University and located right in its shadow. Providence Paranormal used to admit only magi and psychics, but it's been accepting all types of extrahumans ever since Henrietta Thurston became headmistress. There has been trouble since then for students and faculty, leading people to believe dissenters are sabotaging the school.
- **Trout Academy**- A prestigious preparatory school for changelings with magic, recently open to magi and magical shifters. Its campus is located in South County and has been operating in some form or another since Rhode Island Colony was founded.
- **The Under**- The faerie realm. It's been divided into two parts ever since the Sidhe Queen and the Goblin king split up thousands of years ago. Mortals don't age in the Under, but it's a dangerous place for them to be. Getting lost means never being seen again, and it's easy to get indebted to

something nasty while trying to get through or out of the Under.

- **Wolf Messing Prep**- An institute for psychics to learn to control their skills before heading to college.

Events

- **The Big Reveal**- The term used for the 1990s, when the world discovered magic was real and extrahumans existed. The decade was marked with fear as everyone adjusted to the changes. Since the 21st Century, law and technology work for both humans and extrahumans.
- **Boston Internment**- A reaction by Boston government officials to the disappearance and suspected trafficking in extrahumans, especially shifters. All registered extrahumans in Boston lived on barges for close to a month under guard by the Boston Police. The traffickers got their hands on some magical gadgets, rendering the protection useless. Few survived.

THANK YOU!

Thank you for reading! If you loved this book, please leave a review. You can find my other work by clicking the links below, going to **my website** or visiting my **Author Central page**.

For other books by DR Perry please see her Amazon author page.

CONNECT WITH THE AUTHOR

Website: https://www.drperryauthor.com/

Join her newsletter!

Find more of D.R. Perry's books on Amazon.